TACTICAL RESPONSE TEAM • BOOK THREE

SURVIVOR

CINDY BONDS

Scrivenings
PRESS
Quench your thirst for story.
www.ScriveningsPress.com

Published by Scrivenings Press LLC
15 Lucky Lane
Morrilton, Arkansas 72110
https://ScriveningsPress.com

Paperback ISBN 978-1-64917-256-3

eBook ISBN 978-1-64917-257-0

All scriptures are taken from the KING JAMES VERSION (KJV): KING JAMES VERSION, public domain.

Editors: Erin R. Howard and K. Banks

Cover by Linda Fulkerson, bookmarketinggraphics.com

To my dad, Michael Rapp. Whose perseverance in life taught me to work hard and never give up. You will be greatly missed.

PROLOGUE

"What exactly are you accusing me of?" Shelby Durning stared at the pharmacist, face heating at the accusation.

"I'm sorry, but I'm going to have to report this to the police. You can't continue to issue these types of drugs to the same patient."

"But I'm not. This isn't my signature and I've never heard of any of these patients."

"Then why are you here?"

"Someone called my cell asking about refills and I had no idea who the patient was. They told me I could come down and take a look at the script." Shelby picked up the five scripts sitting in front of her. Three were for the same person.

"It's my prescription pad, but I didn't write them. Here, look at my signature." Pulling her license from her purse, she handed it to the pharmacist. "See? It's different."

"Pretty close," the man mumbled. "I still have to call the police."

Shelby nodded. "Thanks for the heads up. I'll put in a complaint. I just don't understand how they got those forms."

"No one has stolen any of your prescription pads?"

"Of course not. I keep them locked up." Her face heated. "Unless ..." Turning on a heel, she rushed from the pharmacy. "It can't be, it just can't be," she whispered.

Once inside her house, she hurried to her office and pulled the keys from her purse. Sliding the chair from the desk, she unlocked the drawer and pulled out the box of prescription pads she'd ordered last week.

"No, no, no, no ..."

Her heart pounded as she stared at the blank pads in the box. The pads were perfect when she accepted the parcel; she had made sure her name was spelled correctly and her med numbers were right. After checking, she stored them here just like she always did, locked up tight.

The only other person that had access to her home was the one person she trusted most.

Standing at the shrill ring of her phone, she rummaged through the bag, wrapping her fingers around the case, and answered.

"Hello?"

"Hey, babe. What're you up to?"

Bile filled her throat as her hand shook. "I'm at home going through some emails."

"You all right?"

"Yeah, just saw an email about a patient," she mumbled, collapsing in the chair and swallowing hard at the reflux.

"Bad news, huh?"

"Very bad."

"I'll be headed home tomorrow. Call me back tonight when you're free and we can talk about my trip. Dallas was awesome."

"Sounds good. I'll call later."

"Love you, Shelby."

She loosened her clenched jaw. "Love you, too."

The call ended and she dropped the phone on the desk. She

stared down at the cushion diamond on her left hand, stomach churning.

"It just can't be," she whispered. "It can't be him."

1

Four Years Later

"Okay, let's just all take it easy."

Focused on the terrified girl, Jeff Powers stood still as her attacker held her shoulders.

"He ... he tried to kill me," the man stuttered as sweat beaded along his brow, his gaze at the body on the floor.

Jeff nodded. "I saw that he tried to hurt you. What's your name?"

The man's voice quivered. "Randal."

"Okay, Randal. Can you hand me the knife? I think that girl is scared, can you release her?"

"I ... I ..." Randal stammered as his arms shook.

"Randal?" Jeff pleaded to get Randal focused. "Look at me."

The man's red-rimmed eyes finally found Jeff.

"I know he attacked you, but I don't want him to die. And I want you to try and keep calm. Can you do that for me?" Jeff glanced at the girl in Randal's grasp. Her sobs echoed in the quiet room as tears streamed down her cheeks. Randal's shaky hand held a knife close to her shoulder.

Once Randal nodded, Jeff scanned the ER. "I need someone to help this man so Randal doesn't get in more trouble."

"I've got it." A woman in a white coat pushed forward and knelt next to the bleeding victim on the floor.

"Okay, good. Randal, this doctor is going to work on him, okay? Because if he dies, you're going to be in a lot of trouble, even more than you're in now."

Randal nodded, his eyes bulging.

"If you could let that girl go, we could go talk to the police."

"You ... you're not the police?" Randal spoke, but his focus was once more on the body on the floor.

"No, I'm not. I work with the police."

The doctor suddenly rushed past Jeff and to the other side of the room, rummaging through boxes and then jogging back to her patient.

You've got to be kidding me.

Jeff rolled his eyes and took a breath. "Look at me, Randal."

"What's she doin'?"

"I'm going to see if I can help, okay?"

Randal nodded emphatically. Taking one last look at the girl in his arms, Jeff frowned. She stood stiffly next to Randal, her sobs silent. Randal's left arm wrapped around her shoulders, his right holding a knife in front of both of them.

"What's going on here?" Jeff whispered as he knelt on the other side of the bleeding body, trying to ease his temper with the doctor.

"This man is about to die. His brachial artery was nicked. It's a slow bleed, but if I don't get him into surgery in the next few minutes, I'll be trying to help a dead man." Her amber eyes glared up at him as she shifted her weight to the injured arm. "You better hurry this up."

Jeff nodded and stood, taking a slow breath. "Okay, Randal, this is what we're going to do." He smiled, pushing out a casual tone. "I'm going to take the knife, and then we're going to walk outside to the officers waiting to talk to you, okay?" He paused only a foot in front of Randal, who was still focused on the floor.

In one quick move, Jeff had Randal's right arm pulled up and twisted, making him drop the knife. A woman rushed forward, yanking the still-frozen girl away as he put Randal on the floor, crying and screaming.

"He tried to kill me!"

"Randal, calm down. I know that." Jeff frowned as he noticed the Semper Fidelis tattoo on his forearm. "Easy, man, we'll get you some help." He quickly pulled some zip ties from his back pocket and used them on Randal's wrists.

Easing the man to his feet, Jeff escorted him to the officers outside, noticing Haiden waiting at the police perimeter. A few officers came forward, snatching Randal from his grip.

"Easy, guys."

"What do you mean easy?" The officer gritted out.

"Someone tried to kill him. I saw the attack. Randal relieved the man of his weapon and then he—"

"Tried to kill a little girl. Yeah, we got that part."

Jeff pushed forward, barely containing his frustration at the officer. "That knife never got close enough to hurt her."

"Jeff."

Haiden's stern voice made Jeff step back and head for the perimeter.

"You, okay?" Haiden stood at attention, rifle across his chest, his face void of emotion.

"Not really, but I'll be fine." He looked around. "Where's everyone else?" His team, the Dallas Tactical Response Team, consisted of former military and police to assist when authorities were spread thin.

"Buck, Evan, and Sergio headed downtown for a supposed shooting rampage. They just radioed in and said it was some kid with a BB gun."

"Where's Danica?"

"She's on the phone with Kyra."

"Everything okay?"

"I guess we'll find out." Haiden frowned, looking over his shoulder for his teammate and fiancé.

"Did you have line of sight?"

Haiden nodded. "Once I heard yelling, I set up across the street. But I wasn't going to shoot a man that wasn't going to do nothing."

"How could you possibly know that?"

"Just like you said to the officers. If he were going to hurt her, that knife would've actually been close enough to do damage. Besides, there were a lot of bodies in that room. My shot would've compromised more people."

Jeff nodded. If Haiden didn't see a reason to end the man's life, he wasn't going to argue. He flexed his hands, then opened up his jacket, letting the mid-morning breeze cool his body.

What a way to start the week. First, the hit and run that pulled him out of church, and now this. If he hadn't shown up to check on the victim from this morning, he wouldn't have been here to help.

How could being at one crime scene so easily lead him to another?

"Mr. Powers?"

Jeff turned to see a few officers motioning for him. Giving a wave, he tuned back to Haiden. "Go ahead and leave. I'll be here for a while."

Haiden nodded and Jeff headed toward the officers, ready to answer more questions.

2

"Get an OR ready. I think I've stopped the bleeding," Dr. Shelby Durning called out as she ran with the gurney, the injured man from the ER lying lifeless as they rushed down the hallway.

"I've got it. You go have a seat."

"I'm fine," she gritted at Dr. Jim Sowers, the on-call surgeon.

"We'll take it from here." RN Talia Masterson gave her a wink, pulling the gurney away from Shelby's hands.

Taking a deep breath, Shelby leaned against the wall, steadying her nerves. The ER wasn't a typical stop in her job. But this? A hostage and an injured man?

"Dr. Durning? There's an officer out here who wants to speak with you."

"Tell him to give me a minute, okay, Sam?"

The orderly nodded and headed back to the front as she closed her eyes.

God, give me strength to face today. No matter the outcome of this situation, help me to see what You want me to see.

It was a daily prayer every morning as she headed to work. But today, she needed to say it twice.

Letting out a deep breath, she slid into one of the open

rooms and scrubbed her hands. Pink-hued water pooled in the silver basin, finally running clear after several washes. Shaking and drying off, she trudged back to the ER, stripping off her jacket and folding the bloody stains into the cloth.

As the doors opened, the smell of antiseptic and bleach smacked her in the face. Sam, along with a few others, were still trying to clean the floor where she had worked on the injured man.

"Dr. Durning?"

Turning to the officer, she nodded.

"We need to go over what happened."

"Sure."

"Is there somewhere else we can speak?"

Motioning the officer back, they walked through the ER doors and found an empty room.

"I just need you to tell me everything from this morning."

Leaning against the counter, Shelby crossed her arms and began. "I was upstairs doing my rounds when I was called to the ER. A patient had requested me at the ER desk."

"Why?"

She shrugged at the officer. "I have no idea."

"YOU'RE NOT LISTENING. Randal was attacked. He defended himself." Jeff argued with the officer in charge.

"Then he used a girl as a hostage."

"I never said that."

"You didn't have to."

Jeff took a step toward the officer, and Buck intervened. "The officer needs your statement, Jeff. This isn't the place to debate intentions."

"And you are?" The officer turned his stern glare to Buck.

Jeff did his best to keep his mouth clamped shut as Buck stepped forward. "Buck Thompson. I'm in charge of the TRT."

Buck turned back to Jeff, pushing him away from the officer. "The last thing we need right now is bad press," he mumbled.

Surveying the room, Jeff nodded. Several of the other witnesses sat in the ER, watching the interaction. Hopefully they hadn't recorded it on their phones and posted it to social media. After the events a few months ago, they were slowly earning back police trust and attempting to mend their tarnished image. A bad confrontation would be a disaster.

"Fine." Jeff motioned to Buck. "I'm going to check on the attacker."

"You mean victim?" the officer scoffed.

"Get the footage from those cameras. If my testimony and the other witness testimony isn't enough for you, then maybe that will be enough proof." Jeff walked away from the officer and toward the surgery wing, Buck on his heels.

"I'm sorry, you can't go in there." A short nurse in scrubs stood from the desk. Her hands planted on her hips as she blocked their entrance into the OR.

"I was here during the stand-off, and I need to know about the injured man that was brought in."

"I'm sorry, but I'm not allowed to give out that information."

"I need to know—"

"It's okay, Talia."

The same doctor from the ER walked around the nurse with a smile. Jeff stood tongue-tied. He hadn't noticed just how pretty she was earlier.

"Buck Thompson. I'm Jeff's boss." Buck stuck out his hand, and the woman shook it with a nod.

"I'm Dr. Shelby Durning. I was here during the hostage situation."

"Jeff Powers."

"Mr. Powers." Shelby returned Jeff's handshake. "The patient is in surgery. We'll know more later, but he lost a lot of blood."

Jeff frowned. "I was hoping for better news."

"Me too. Good job out there, by the way, getting Randal's

attention." Shelby pocketed her hand as a smile spread across her face.

"It was ... an intense situation. I'm glad we had someone here that could take care of it."

"From what I've heard, Jeff's lucky you were there to step up, help keep that man alive."

She grinned bigger as her gaze turned to Buck. "That's what I do."

Her smile was amazing. But then again, so were her eyes and the way her eyebrow perked ...

"Excuse me. I've got a call," Buck mumbled and bumped Jeff's arm as he walked past.

Jeff cleared his throat. "You mind if we go over a few things? I just want to know what you saw."

"Sure thing. How about we step away from the OR?"

Jeff grinned at the beautiful doctor, following her to another corridor, his mind on overdrive.

Man, where was his focus?

3

"They just seem bent on labeling the guy, I guess," Jeff Powers, the negotiator from the ER incident mumbled, his eyes searching over the area behind her.

Dr. Shelby During nodded. "He did have that girl by the shoulder, but I agree, I think Randal was in shock himself." She paused as her name came over the speaker. "Sorry, that's me. I've got to go."

"Oh, okay. Well, thanks." Mr. Powers grinned as he held out his hand. "Till I see you again."

She shook his hand with a smirk. "Okay ..." she drew out the word as Mr. Powers turned.

He headed to the front doors, and she let out a sigh as she made her way to the back elevators.

He didn't even ask? He'd already gone over what happened several times, prolonging the conversation. It seemed as if he were building up to something, and as much of a recluse as she'd become, coffee with a guy like him sounded appealing.

Bright blue eyes, tall and thin, with dirty blonde hair swept back. Jeff Powers was an attractive man. With his square shoulders and great smile, he was the kind of guy that would turn any woman's head.

"He probably already has a girlfriend," she mumbled as she left the open elevator and stepped onto the sixth floor.

Slinging on the borrowed scrub jacket, she took the offered chart from the nurses' desk. Leaning against the counter, she studied the lab results.

"Dr. Durning? There's a phone call for you."

She took the offered phone. "Dr. Durning."

"Oh, um, hi."

Smirking, she held in her chuckle. "Mr. Powers. Why're you acting surprised when you called me?"

"I didn't realize it would be so quick. I was kinda thinking I'd back out."

"Of what?"

"Just wondering if we could get some coffee sometime?"

She paused, mouth open but nothing coming out.

"See, if I was there right now, I could at least judge your reaction. But on the phone, I'm not sure what just happened."

"I'm sorry. I'm working late today and on call tomorrow. I would hate to meet you and then have to leave."

"Oh. That's okay ..."

"Just ..." Speaking at the same time, she winced.

"Go ahead, I'm sorry."

"I was going to say, if you give me your number, I can let you know about tomorrow. If you still want to, that is." She pulled out her phone.

"Of course, I'd still like to go. But I understand you're probably really busy."

"I am."

She left the rest unsaid. Her job was overwhelming. The long hours and on-call days through holidays and vacations left little time to find a relationship that could evolve into something serious. Not that she'd tried all that hard lately.

"You ready?"

Shaking away old memories, she opened her contact list. "Yes."

After rattling off his number, he paused. "Unless I'm out on a call, you can reach me anytime."

"Okay, sounds good."

The nurse tapped on the chart with a frown.

"I'm sorry, I've got to go. I'll let you know about tomorrow."

"Sounds great. Bye."

The call ended and Shelby dropped the phone in the jacket pocket and put the receiver back on the base at the desk. Following the nurse down the hallway, she pushed Jeff Power's blue eyes from her mind, ignoring her anxiousness at the thought of coffee with him.

JEFF PARKED the SUV in the Tactical Response Team garage and let out a groan.

Asking out the doctor that helped save a man's life during a hostage negotiation probably wasn't the best idea.

Shaking his head, he slid from the seat and slammed the door. It had been a few months since he had been on a date. A blind date that he begrudgingly relented to when Evan said Bexley had several very interesting and talented friends.

Although it hadn't been a train wreck, there was zero interest, and he was pretty certain it went both ways. Especially since the woman had never called or even texted him for a follow-up.

Walking down the hallway, he tossed his bag into the equipment room, then headed for the kitchen. The whole team was gathered in the living area, minus Sergio.

"I heard you had an interesting morning."

He frowned at Evan before opening the fridge for a bottle of water. "You could say that. I went to check on the hit-and-run victim from this morning and ended up in a stand-off."

"So, the guy had a knife but wasn't threatening?" Evan turned to Jeff from the barstool, Bexley at his side.

"Almost. He had his arm wrapped around a young girl's shoulders, the knife in his other hand. I'm not saying that's okay, but I can't believe he intended to hurt her. The attack on his life just escalated whatever was wrong and had him in the ER. No one could tell me why he was even there. I'll check with the detective in the morning and see if he'll even talk to me."

Buck let out a huff and headed to his office, slamming the door. That was odd.

"What about the guy that was in the hit and run?" Evan asked.

"He's going to be okay. Broke a leg, but from what the ER doctor said, he was stable."

"At least that turned out good," Haiden mumbled from behind him.

Jeff tugged on Danica's arm and headed to the conference room in the back of the office. He grabbed the doorknob, pausing as Haiden followed Dani into the room.

"What's up with Buck?" He shut the door. "He's got something going on."

"Maybe he's worried about bad press. I heard you weren't all that kind to the officers as you were being questioned." Haiden's slow drawl pushed out the words as he wrapped an arm around Dani.

Jeff sighed and fell back into the chair. "Thanks, man," he mumbled. "They were making accusations, creating a preset that would become truth and they won't look any further. To figure out how Randal got into that situation, they have to figure out why he was attacked in the first place."

Dani shrugged. "I agree. But it's not our job, right?"

"Yeah."

"So, what else happened?"

His eyebrow rose. "What's that supposed to mean?"

"Buck mentioned a doctor." Haiden gave a smirk and Jeff stood, nodding as he headed for the door.

"Okay, I'm done. Thanks for the insight."

Danica jumped up and took ahold of his arm. "Oh, come on! Give me something."

Pausing, he glanced over her head at Haiden. "I asked her out."

"Asked ... the doctor? Really?"

"Yeah," he mumbled.

"I can't believe it. It's been forever since *you* asked someone out."

He paced, nervously rubbing the back of his neck.

"Did she say no?"

"She couldn't tonight because she's working late and on call tomorrow. She said she hated to sit down and then have to leave ..." he trailed off.

"So, what's the plan?" Danica sat back down with Haiden.

Jeff shrugged. "She asked for my number and said she'd call."

"Good. That's a great step."

Jeff kept pacing, then paused to face her. "I—"

"Don't do it, Jeff."

"Do what?"

"Sit. Now." She glared until he finally collapsed into a chair. "You're already thinking about backing out. She'd be a good fit for you. She's mature and has her own career."

Jeff cracked his knuckles as he blew out a heavy breath. "In other words, she's not Meline. Is that what you're saying?" He cut his eyes to Haiden and then back to her.

Danica shrugged. "Yes, but then again, you two are a lot older than you and Meline were. You should at least give her a shot. If she calls, great, if not, then you tried and can move on. But you need to move on."

"Yeah, yeah. It's easy for everyone around here to say that."

Dani pulled her phone from her pocket. "Hang on, it's Kyra. She had a job interview this morning and is really excited."

As Danica left, Jeff raked his fingers through his hair.

"It's not easy to say that."

Jeff's eyes cut to Haiden. "What?"

Haiden leaned in on his knees. "Don't think any of this was easy. You were there."

Jeff's jaw clenched, his heart pounding at the memory of Dani being in trouble.

"Almost losing her was the worst day of my life and I'll never be able to forget it. This hasn't been easy. But it's been the best decision I've ever made."

"I've been there too," Jeff muttered.

Haiden nodded, his eyes narrowing.

"Not the time." Jeff stood and headed for the door and to his room.

Talking about Meline wasn't something he did. Danica was there; she saw what happened first-hand. But when dissecting every single bad decision he made, it became real all over again. It's not like thoughts of her didn't flood his memory over and over.

As he leaned against his desk, he blew out a deep breath. Yanking the drawer open, he stared at the gold band still sitting in its spot. He couldn't get rid of it, but he couldn't put it away either. It was a great reminder of why he stepped away from serious personal interactions, why he never allowed himself to get too close.

So why would he ask out the doc like that?

Slamming the drawer, he grabbed gym shorts from the pile of clothes on his bed to change into. This day was already spinning into chaos and a workout was the only thing that might actually help.

4

"I've got a guy that can make it happen."

Pouring himself a drink, Louis Roltz perched on the edge of his 1910 mahogany writing desk. "Look, I don't care about your guy. I care about keeping certain people happy. The last *guy* you knew disappeared and is still a loose end I expect you to handle. You've been paid. I want results." Disconnecting the call, Louis tossed the phone aside.

His hired help, although efficient in the past, was proving a disappointment in this situation. And this time, he could lose everything. The election, his wealth, his freedom, it was all in jeopardy.

Staring at the muted T.V. on the wall, he grinned as the story of his halfway house for young men was featured on the newsreel.

After all the planning, the pushing, it was coming together. The primaries were in a few months, and the media already had him ahead by several votes. Once he came out on top, all he had to do was wait until November and he'd be the new mayor.

"It's going to be a grand day," he muttered, sitting on his couch and lighting his cigar.

JEFF STOOD at the detective's desk, face hot and jaw aching from keeping his mouth shut.

"Mr. Randal Goodwin isn't giving us anything to go on. He said he's not denying what he did." Detective Fredrick shrugged. "I have to charge him with attacking the girl and, depending on what my boss says, that guy, Terry Quarters."

"Has Randal said why he was at the ER this morning?"

"Nope. Like I said, he's not interested in talking."

Jeff shook his head. "There's something else going on with all of this. Why would someone attack him while sitting in an ER?"

"Look, we've gone through Mr. Goodwin's and Mr. Quarters' lives, but so far, nothing intersects. Quarters' been arrested a few times. A couple of loitering charges, and we picked him up last year for a disorderly charge. He'd been in a bar drinking and some guy took a swing at him and lost." Fredrick's sat down. "He only served a few months and was released."

"Terry Quarters brought a huge buck knife into the ER. He had no holster, and it's too big to simply carry around for protection. Why did he have it?"

"Mr. Powers, I can understand that you feel for Goodwin. I know you work with former military types. But Goodwin is going to be charged for holding that girl hostage. Maybe he can get a good lawyer and pull some kind of insanity plea."

"He's not insane. He was distressed after being attacked and reacted badly. By the time I turned around, Randal was using defensive tactics to gain the weapon and ended up hitting the other guy's arm. I saw him take that knife from Quarters."

"I get it. But unless Randal tells me why Terry Quarters attacked him and gives me some kind of reasoning behind the situation, I've got nothing else to go on."

"Even with the video evidence and the commentary from the witnesses? It's not enough to see that he was defending himself?"

Fredricks shrugged. "I've not received the video yet. It's in the ER, so we've got some red tape to cut. But based on testimony, I think we can get the attack on Terry Quarters down to self-defense. The girl he had a hold of is another story. Once I get the video, I'll have a better idea of what the DA will want to do."

"Thanks anyway," Jeff murmured as he gave a nod and turned to leave.

None of it made sense. Why would Randal not want to explain what happened in the ER and clear his name? And why would Terry Quarters attack a man sitting there if he didn't know him?

As Jeff slid into the SUV, his brain rushed to connect the dots. Something was missing, and there was no way he could just let it go. His training, from the FBI to Homeland, had been his job for almost a decade. Dissect every aspect of the case, find the motive, find the answers.

Swallowing the lump in his throat, he ignored the prodding in the back of his mind. Sometimes bringing everything to light didn't make it easier to fix; it made it all much more complex.

He yanked the phone from his pocket and checked the screen. For some ridiculous reason, he hoped the pretty doctor texted him about tomorrow. Although anxious about actually going on a date, her smile and character intrigued him. Any woman that would risk so much in the middle of a possible hostage standoff had his interest.

Letting out a sigh, he started the car and headed back to the office. Buck was a great teacher and trainer. His experience gave them a step up in tough situations, an edge that made them prepared and ready for action.

But today, Jeff's mind was everywhere but on training.

5

"Finally," Shelby mumbled and leaned against the back of the elevator.

Her ten-hour workday had just wrapped up after midnight and she could finally go home. Pulling her phone from the jacket pocket, she shook her head with a smile. Jeff Power's number still sat on her screen.

"Maybe coffee won't be so bad," she muttered, sliding the phone back into her pocket.

Stepping off the elevator on the ground floor, she edged around a large man pacing the hallway. "Excuse me? Can I help you?"

He turned, eyes narrowed. "I have a friend here but they won't tell me where he is."

She motioned to the nurses' station. "If you go ask—"

"I already did."

With a nod, she pulled her keys from her purse. "I'm sorry. But if you're not on the list to see him, we're not legally allowed to give any information."

As she stepped around him, a sharp pain hit her side and his hand squeezed her upper arm.

"They might not help, but I think you can," he murmured. "Let's head upstairs."

"But I ..." she desperately strained, looking to the nurses' station for help.

The elevator doors opened and he shoved her inside.

"I really don't think I can tell you where he is," she whispered, fighting the pain pulsing through her side.

"Either you find him, or this night will end much worse than you can imagine." His large frame pushed her against the wall, body odor and alcohol wafting in the air as she avoided his eyes.

Turning her head, she nodded. "Okay, um, how badly is he injured?"

"What does that matter?" he sneered.

"If I know what's wrong, we can go to the correct floor."

"Don't know. He just didn't show up. Apparently, his morning didn't go as planned," his eyes narrowed as he looked her over, his jaw clenched.

With a shaky hand, she pushed the six button. "Let's start with critical care and see if he's there."

The man backed up slightly, his dark eyes still staring. As the doors opened, she slid her hand into her pocket.

"What're you doing?" he hissed and grabbed her elbow.

"I ... I have to put on my badge." She stammered. "If it's not on, they'll know something's wrong. We have to wear them on the floor."

Before pulling the badge out, she tapped at the face of the phone in her pocket.

Please let it call out, Lord. Please!

Putting on her ID, she led the man to the nurses' station. "What's the man's name?"

"Terry Quarters."

JEFF GROGGILY REACHED to the nightstand, searching for the lit-up and vibrating phone. Pulling it to his ear, a muffled scraping sounded.

Must be a misdial. Squinting in the darkness at the bright screen, he frowned at the number and the unknown name.

"You're going to do what?"

Jeff jumped up at the sound of Dr. During's high-pitched voice. "I'm not going to help you kill him."

He started to speak when a deep voice echoed in the background.

"Tell me why he's here."

"This morning at the ER ..." her voice trailed off.

"You either help me wake him up, or you'll be the one in that bed."

Muting his side of the call and snatching the landline, he called Buck.

"What?"

"I think there's something going down at the hospital."

"Think?" Buck groaned. "It's after midnight, Jeff. This better be more than think."

"I just received a phone call from the doctor at the ER. The call is muffled like it's in her pocket. I just heard her say I'm not going to let you kill him. And then a second ago, a man's voice said she can either help or she'll be the one in the bed."

"Get the others up. I'll put in a call and see if anyone else is on the way."

Jeff headed down the hallway as he listened to the voices murmuring through the phone. He banged on Evan's door.

Hair on end, Evan answered. "What?"

"Get Haiden up and call in Sergio and Danica." Jeff filled Evan in on the situation.

"Yeah, give me five," Evan muttered as he snatched his phone from the charger on the wall.

Jeff hustled back to his room, dressed, and paced the entryway waiting for Buck. A muffled thud followed by a high-pitched yelp sounded on the line, and his face heated as his fist tightened.

Buck entered the building. "Okay, let's go. The police said they had a call from a concerned nurse but haven't heard back from the guard they radioed to investigate. What've you heard?"

Jeff shrugged. "Nothing more specific, but I'm certain they're at the hospital."

"Then let's load up."

Evan appeared, sliding his phone into his back pocket. "Danica and Sergio will meet us there."

Haiden stepped into the hallway from the locker room, geared up and rifle ready.

"Let's go," Jeff mumbled.

Piling into one vehicle, Buck drove to the hospital. Jeff kept the phone speaker on but muted.

"Just stop, you're going to kill him!" Shelby's voice strained and he gripped the door.

"Do we know what room she's in?"

"No, but if a nurse called it in, she must've seen something that bothered her. Maybe she'll know what room they went into."

As they drove, Evan handed out earpieces to everyone. Jeff looked over his shoulder to the back seat. "Haiden?"

"If you give me a direction, then a floor number, I can get set up." He pulled the sniper rifle upright in his arm.

Parking in the barren lot, Jeff grabbed his rifle from the back and they raced through the ER entrance. An officer waited at the doors, and Buck took lead. "TRT, we called about a possible situation. You checked it out?"

"Yeah, but the doc was alone in the room with the patient. She said everything was good."

"What room number?"

"602."

Haiden walked to the map on the wall. "East side. There's a

parking garage there." He turned and took off. "Keep me in the loop!" He called over his shoulder.

"Let's go." Jeff led the team up the stairs, unwilling to wait for the elevator.

Once on the sixth floor, he led the team into the hallway.

Sergio stopped at the nurses' station. "Ma'am, you need to clear all unnecessary personnel."

"As soon as that monitor goes off, every available nurse and doctor will be in here to try and resuscitate him. You won't get away." Shelby's voice echoed as they headed quietly down the hallway toward 602.

"Yes, I will." The man's tone escalated, becoming more unstable and prompting Jeff to pick up his pace.

"Hey, I've got a plan." Danica's voice filled his ear and he halted. "Get back here."

"Dani?"

"We need to give Haiden time to get in place."

Jeff clenched his teeth a moment. "Yeah, okay," he mumbled.

Jeff and Buck turned back to where they entered, leaving Sergio and Evan watching the door. As they came around the corner, Danica came out of the bathroom dressed in scrubs.

"I'll go in and assess the situation."

"Dani."

"Jeff, stop. We don't know what's going on in that room."

"She's with a man."

Jeff turned to a nurse who stood pale-faced at the nurses' station. "Did you see him?"

"There's this guy with her, big, intimidating. Shelby acted nervous and worried. Normally we don't allow visitors at this time of night, but she insisted. That's why I called it in."

Danica bumped his arm. "We need in there. This will work." She snatched a stethoscope and a notepad from the nurses' desk, then jogged down the hallway, pulling a small machine with her.

"Thanks. You need to leave." Jeff motioned the nurse to the elevator, then turned to the hallway. "Haiden, are you ready?"

"I need another second."

"Hurry." He took a deep breath as they once more stalked down the hallway.

"OH, sorry doc, didn't know you were here."

Shelby spun around, trying to find some words before the man killed both of them. "Um, yes. This is Mr. Quarter's brother and he was concerned so, so he called me."

The woman in scrubs was unfamiliar. Where was her badge? Who was she?

"Well, sir, I'm sure you were really glad the doc was at the ER this morning, huh?" The nurse gave a big grin as she approached the patient, awkwardly pulling the blood pressure machine behind her.

The attacker nodded, his body pushing behind Shelby. His grip tightened on the back of her coat. The nurse fixed the blood pressure cuff on the man in the bed. It was lopsided.

"You know, having such dedicated personnel is so important. Knowing someone is going to be there and ready when you need them, it's priceless." The nurse looked up and winked.

Shelby managed a nod.

"Is there anything else you need, doc?"

Shelby's mouth dropped open as a pain seared into her back. "No, no I'm fine. I think he had a few more questions, then we'll finish up and let Terry rest."

"Okay, I'll be back with his pain medicine. We don't want him waking just yet, right?"

Shelby swallowed hard at the burning ache in her side. "That's right."

Before leaving through the door, the woman in the scrubs lingered a moment, her eyes shifting from Shelby to her attacker.

"That was too close." The man hissed into her ear. "Either

find me a quick way to take care of him, or you're going to have to watch him bleed out again."

"I won't help you kill him." She turned to her captor, holding her side. "I don't care what you do to me. I won't be a part of this."

The man let out a deep-throated chuckle. "Then what good are you?"

A thud sounded from behind and the man grabbed her throat, yanking her toward him. Straining for breath and fighting against the hand wrapped around her throat, Shelby opened her eyes to see the barrel of a gun.

6

"You're done. You might as well quit now and live." Jeff focused on the man standing behind Shelby, his arm now wrapped around her waist and using her as a shield.

"You've got no shot, man." The attacker pressed the knife to her neck.

"Get him still." Haiden's voice whispered through the earpiece.

"You don't have a way out. And your friend will live to talk about how you paid him to kill off Randal."

"What? You know nothin'!"

"I know that you're here to find out what happened. Why this man," Jeff motioned to Terry Quarters. "... didn't kill Randal Goodwin."

The attacker stilled, a wide-eyed glare focused on Jeff's gun. Dr. Durning was at least a foot shorter, her body already sliding down to the ground.

"But if you put down the knife and let us talk this out, we can come to some kind of compromise. You've not killed anyone yet." Jeff eased the anger in his voice.

"What you're going to do is back out of this room and let me go with the good doctor here."

"Ready," Haiden answered.

Jeff's eyes finally met Shelby's, and he nodded.

A shot rang out as glass shattered, the man's body flying backward and pulling Shelby's torso with him.

Jeff snatched her up before she hit the ground, sweeping her to the side so Buck could clear the body. "I've got you."

Her screams softened as she eased and her arm gripped his neck.

"It's okay, Shelby. I've got you."

Rushing down the hallway with her in his arms, he slid into the open elevators.

"I ... I'm okay," she whispered between sobs.

"I'm taking you to the ER."

"Jeff, put me down. I'm okay." She tugged on his neck. "I can walk," she whispered as he gently eased her to the ground, keeping hold of her waist. "I ..." she trailed off as her eyes shifted to his arm, a dark red blood stain smeared across his sleeve. "Are you hurt?"

"That's yours, Shelby."

The doors opened and he pulled her through, sweeping her up once again and setting her on the first empty bed he saw.

"Shelby? That was you up there?"

Jeff tried to step back and allow the doctor room to check her out, but Shelby's hand clamped down on his.

"Wait." Her wide, red eyes stared at him.

"I'll be right outside, okay?" Jeff gave her a wink. "I'll be here after they check you out."

"Oh, okay," she mumbled.

Stepping away and through the door, Jeff barely managed to keep from busting back inside. After seeing her in so much danger, the fear etched across her face ... his heart pounded as he swallowed the lump in his throat.

God, heal her. Help her find a way to deal with all of this.

7

———

"Is she going to be okay?"

Jeff paced the hallway, ignoring the fact Danica had risked her life going into the room with a knife-wielding psycho. "Yeah, the doctor said the cut on her back was pretty deep, but they should be about done by now. I think the aftereffects are going to haunt her worse than the cut."

"I'm sure it will. But I think you can help her through that, right?"

Jeff shook his head at her smirk. "That was a risky move, going in there like that."

"Haiden needed time to set up, and we needed eyes." Dani shrugged. "Besides, between you and Haiden, I know I'm good."

Jeff glanced up to see Haiden rushing down the hallway. "I guess you get to explain that to him."

Dani turned and met Haiden with a hug.

After her kidnapping, the walls had fallen down for both Haiden and Danica. They were finally able to admit what everyone else saw so clearly. Come to think of it, it was the same with Bexley and Evan. And now they were planning a wedding.

Why did it always have to come down to a life-ending event before people figured out what they really wanted?

The doors opened, and the doctor who had assessed Shelby exited.

"Is she okay?"

"Yes, she is." Shelby came out in a scrub top from behind the doctor. "Thanks, Charles. But I'm ready to go."

"Yes, ma'am." Charles nodded with a chuckle as he headed to the nurses' station.

Jeff stood mesmerized once again. Pushing past him, Danica smiled at Shelby.

"You're one tough lady. Glad everything turned out well."

Shelby took a breath, opening her mouth, then shutting it again. Wiping her eyes, she nodded. "Thanks so much for coming. I ... I didn't know what else to do and I—"

Danica stepped closer. "By the way, I'm Danica. I work with Jeff."

Shelby managed a smile. "I wondered why I didn't recognize you. You do great work. Maybe you need a career change?"

Danica laughed out loud. "Nope. I'm good where I'm at."

Jeff motioned to the hallway. "My boss, Buck. He wants to interview you before you go home. Is that okay?"

"Um, yeah, sure. Let's get it over with." Shelby nervously pulled at the purse in her hands.

He led the way to the waiting area. "Let's have a seat."

Letting out a long breath, Shelby eased into the chair. He sat down next to her.

"How're you feeling?"

"Not great, but then again, things could be worse." Shelby forced a smile as she nervously gripped her bag in her lap.

"Someone brought you your purse?"

"Yes, I asked one of the nurses to get it for me. I left it at the nurses' station before I ..." she trailed off and clenched her hands.

Jeff nodded, trying to find a way to fill the awkward silence. He leaned forward on his knees, rubbing the back of his neck.

"You know, when you said you'd call, that was the last thing I was expecting."

She wiped some stray tears as they rolled off her cheek. "Oh, Jeff. I'm so sorry. This whole thing is a mess, and I—"

"I didn't mean it like that." He gently touched her wrist. "Look, I'm trying to ease the situation a bit, but obviously, I'm blowing it."

"No, you're not." She took a deep breath. "With all the adrenaline and even though I passed out earlier, it's not wearing off like I thought it would and I'm just shaky."

"You passed out?"

Her eyes finally met his as she swiped her cheek. "Well, my back hurt and I was just—" her mouth hung open for a moment before she closed it, blinked, and moved her focus away from him. "This has been a long day."

She pulled her long, dusty blonde hair from her face and he smiled.

"I'm sorry to make you wait, Dr. Durning."

Jeff stood as Buck walked up. Realizing he was still gripping her wrist, he dropped it as she stood next to him.

"This is Detective Alton. He wanted to sit in on the interview. Please, have a seat." Holding her side, Shelby lowered back into the chair.

"I'll make this as quick as possible. I just need to know what happened from the time you clocked out until now."

With a few slow breaths, her eyes jutted between the two men. "I had finished my charts and left them at the nurses' station. When I left the elevator, I saw a man pacing and asked if he needed help, and he said he was there to see someone. I suggested he go to the nurses' station and he said he already did, but they wouldn't help him. I told him I couldn't either if he wasn't on the patient's list. That's when he stepped close with something sharp in his hand.

"I mean, I'm usually really good at paying attention to my

surroundings and everything. But I was thrown off since we were still in the building and the nurse's station was in sight."

"It's not your fault. It's just not possible to know every situation at all times." Jeff leaned forward on his knees.

"He—he said he needed my help." A shudder moved through her and he fought the instinct to reach out. "I went to the sixth floor since that's where I left. I thought they might find it odd I came back.

"When I went to get my badge, I told him I had to have it on or the nurses would notice. That's when I hit, or I hoped I hit, the call button on my phone." She managed to look up at him again. "Your name was still on the screen. It was the last time I was actually on my phone tonight and I had just slid it into my pocket. I tried to make sure the nurse was involved, asking for the patient's room."

"She noticed, that's what sent the officer to the door. That was a smart move." He offered a grin as she wiped her cheek.

"I wanted to say something when the officer showed, but the man hid and the officer didn't come into the room and I ..." she took a breath. "I was so surprised the patient was the man from this morning. When he noticed I recognized who it was in the bed, he ordered me to tell him what happened. He was mad and wanted to wake up the patient. I did what I could, but the man was heavily sedated."

Jeff looked up to Buck, who nodded. It seemed there was much more going on with the man that attacked Randal.

"Thanks, Dr. Durning."

"Call me Shelby."

Buck nodded. "I just need your address and phone number. Detective? Anything else?"

"Just one. Did you recognize the man that abducted you?"

"No, I've never seen him before."

"He didn't say why he wanted that specific patient's room? Nothing that would explain why he was there or the connection to the patient from this morning?"

"No, he just wanted to wake him up, and when that didn't work, he said he'd kill him," she whispered.

Detective Alton stood with a nod and left the room, phone in hand.

"We'll call if there's anything else we might need, okay?" Buck stood.

"Okay, thanks."

"Do you have someone to come pick you up?"

She shook her head at Buck's question. "Oh, I'll be fine."

"No, I'll drive you." Jeff held out his hand as Buck nodded and left.

It took her longer than he liked for her to finally take his hand and stand with a groan.

"Your back?"

"Yeah, I'm just sore. I feel like I've been thrown around."

"You were." He frowned as she shook her head.

"I can drive. They didn't give me any pain medicine besides some Tylenol."

"No, you can't. It's protocol." He held out his other hand and she huffed as she pulled her keys from her purse.

Before giving them over, she looked up at him for a minute, those big amber eyes studying him. "Are you sure it's protocol?"

"Yes, ma'am. Besides, I wouldn't hit on a woman that had just been through what you've been through tonight." He let a smirk out at her discerning eye.

"Fine." She dropped them in his hand, and he stepped to the side to allow her to lead the way.

He texted Evan to come pick him up at the doctor's address as they made their way to the outer doors. She paused, scanning the darkness, her body tensing as he stepped in closer.

"Come on." He wrapped his arm gently around her shoulders and even though she stiffened, he kept his body against hers and in step as they made their way to her car.

"I'm not usually so worried," she muttered.

"You've been through a lot tonight. Give yourself time to

deal. You'll be nervous the first couple of times you head out alone, then it'll ease up."

"You act like you know what you're talking about."

They paused at her door as he held it open for her, and she faced him.

"I just have a lot of experience in this field." He forced a smile as she carefully climbed into the large SUV, then he shut her door.

The silence lingered in the car and he let it. Trying to clear the air like last time and sounding foolish wasn't happening again.

"So, how long have you been working with the police?"

He smirked. "I've worked in law enforcement for ten years."

"I'm guessing by that answer, you mean you've been in different arenas."

He nodded with a smile. "Yes."

"And you don't want to elaborate?"

He glanced over to see her intently watching him. "Can I ask you a question first?"

"You can ask."

"What is it you're looking for?"

"What do you mean?"

He grinned at her playful tone. "You're sure looking for something and if you just tell me, maybe I can actually give you an answer."

The silence lingered again, and as they came to a stop light, he looked over to see her staring out the window.

"Shelby?"

"Yes?"

He sighed as she kept her focus outside. "I worked primarily with the FBI when I first started and then with Homeland for a short time. The past two years, I've been with Buck and the TRT."

"I'm assuming you have specialized training as well?"

He nodded. "I did extensive profile work with Homeland."

He smiled as he heard her chuckle. "Did that answer your questions?"

"Almost."

He pulled into her driveway as silence consumed the car.

She pushed the button on the rearview mirror so he could pull into the garage. After opening her door, he followed her inside, watching as she pushed the alarm code and closed the garage door.

Her home was quaint, not as big as he imagined for a doctor. It was homey and lived-in, and the smell of cinnamon and spice permeated the air.

"Oh, how're you going to get home?" She paused, slowly easing the coat off her shoulders and arms.

"My ride should be here any second." With a nod, she turned to go into the kitchen.

"Hey, your back. It's bleeding." He stepped in behind her and she turned with a frown.

"I'm sure it's just from being stitched up."

"You sure?" He clenched his jaw, doubting it was something so small. "That spot is a lot bigger than just a drop from being stitched up."

"It's fine. I'll check it later." She forced a smile as his phone went off. "I guess that's your ride."

He nodded as he shoved his hands into his pockets and watched her for a moment as a standoff ensued. She crossed her arms and studied him back, making him chuckle.

"And what are you searching for, Mr. Powers?"

"Nothing specific. Just wondering why you won't let me check your back. You might've busted a stitch climbing in and out of your car."

"No, I think it would be hurting much worse if it tore." Pushing past him, she maneuvered to the front and turned on the porch light. "Thanks so much, Jeff, for everything."

"You don't have to thank me. I'm just glad I showed up when I did." He made his way to the door, which she quickly unlocked and opened for him. "However, if you did want to call me for any other reason, as you can see, I'm pretty quick to respond." He smiled as she finally smiled back.

"I'll keep that in mind. But now, you have my number too." She raised her eyebrow.

"Yes, I do. Take care, Shelby. I don't expect to find you at the hospital tomorrow, right?"

"Probably not tomorrow." She narrowed her eyes and he paused, thinking he had just crossed a line.

"Good night."

"Good night, Jeff."

He nodded and she gave a quick wave as he headed outside to Evan.

"Took you long enough, good grief."

Jeff slid into the seat and grinned. "You could've sent Buck or Haiden if you had other plans."

"Yeah, well, Haiden and Dani are otherwise detained and I don't know where Buck went."

"Something's going on with him. Ever since this morning, he's been off."

"He's got a lot going on. We've got bridges to mend with the police and that guy running for mayor is still making comments. Even after everything we went through with Danica, public opinion is still important and Roltz has a lot of people swayed."

"I guess so."

The fact mayoral runner-up Louis Roltz was still gunning for the TRT didn't make sense. But it also didn't stop the media from suddenly discovering situations and past occurrences of all the members of the TRT and their families.

Kyra, Danica's sister, had been injured in a hit and run prior to Danica's kidnapping three months ago. Suddenly, Kyra was all over social media, accused of using drugs and being caught in the middle of a drug war.

Although she's been sober for two years, several reporters acted as if Danica should be considered unfit for duty because of the family connection. Haiden even mentioned his mother had to chase off reporters from his father's hospital room. They were asking questions about Haiden's childhood as the police escorted them out.

"If we don't get ahead of all of this now, we're going to be right back where we were three months ago. Dodging reporters' questions and trying to keep from looking incompetent."

"Ahead of what exactly?" Evan turned long enough to set a stare.

"There are still some people unaccounted for."

"Just one. Dale Fletcher."

Jeff flipped his phone over and over on his knee. "If we can find him, I think we'll have a connection that will close the gap on all this media nonsense, Louis Roltz and his hatred of the TRT."

"Enough about Roltz, how's the doc?"

Jeff groaned. "You too, huh?"

Evan shrugged. "I saw you go in and come out with her, the look on your face, you were scared."

"Scared? Really?"

"Just telling you what I saw."

"Yeah, well, if it weren't for Haiden, I'm not sure how that would've ended," Jeff mumbled as he stared into the darkness.

It had been a trial, one he wouldn't be forgetting any time soon. The look on Shelby's face, the scream as the shot fired, and her attacker pulling her down from behind had made for a terrifying scene.

"She's going to have a hard time getting over that," Evan mumbled.

"Yeah." Jeff sighed. "She's tough, but after what happened, she's going to struggle."

"What're you going to do about it?"

Jeff swung his gaze to Evan. "I guess it depends on if she'll let me."

Evan chuckled. "Don't give her a choice. Step up and help."

"That's what you did, huh?"

"We're engaged, aren't we?" Evan's grin spread across his face as they pulled into the TRT garage. "I'm just saying if you want to help, be available."

Jeff slid from the truck and let out a sigh. Of all the words he could come up with to describe himself, available wouldn't be one of them. But if she would accept his help, then yeah, he'd make himself available.

However, based on tonight's reaction, she didn't seem all that free herself.

Man, it was going to be a long night.

8

Monday Morning

"You're up."

Jeff yawned as he sat down at the kitchen island. Dani grinned as she stood at the stove cooking breakfast.

"You ready for a full day?"

"Full day of what?"

"Buck has a schedule of drills planned. I think after last night, he wants us to discuss and go over entering small spaces."

"Yeah, after you went inside a room with no visibility and stood face to face with a crazy man and his hostage."

Dani stuck her tongue out at him.

"Trust me, we've discussed it." Haiden's low drawl sounded from behind Jeff.

"Haiden had eyes."

"Not right then," Haiden muttered as he poured himself some coffee.

Danica gave Haiden a kiss on the cheek. "I guess we need the practice then."

"*You do*," Jeff mumbled, standing to grab his own coffee mug. "Where's Bexley and Evan?"

"Bex is out shopping and will be meeting us there. I don't know where Evan is." Dani leaned against the counter.

"When are we supposed to be there?"

"An hour," Haiden answered.

A strange silence filled the space and Jeff frowned. "Spill. What's going on?"

Haiden shrugged.

"Dani?"

"I just wanted to know how your evening with the doctor went."

Jeff rolled his eyes. "Just fine. But I'm not sure that's it." Cutting his eyes between the two, it was more than obvious something else was up. "You sure that's it?"

Haiden only sipped his coffee, his gaze on Dani.

"I talked to Kyra yesterday."

"I remember."

She huffed. "She starts her new job tomorrow. It's a receptionist position so she doesn't have to worry about walking around a lot. But she did get a new walking cast."

"I'm glad she was able to find something and that she can get around better. What else?"

Dani shrugged. "Nothing. I've just been curious about you and the doctor. She's very pretty."

Jeff stood. "I don't have time to sit here and wait for you to spill whatever it is you don't want to talk about with me. If Buck is planning drills, it's going to be a long day."

Coffee in hand, Jeff headed down the hallway to his room. For some reason, Danica kept forgetting what he used to do for a living. Although reading her, judging her reactions, that was easy. She was practically his sister. Haiden was tougher, but there was obviously something else they were not saying.

Pulling his phone from the charger, he stared at the blank screen.

"She's probably still asleep."

It's not like she'd be calling him already, not after what she'd been through. But that nagging pull in his chest left him wondering if he should text her and make sure she was all right.

Letting out a groan, he grabbed some clothes and headed to the shower to hopefully wake himself up. If Buck was all worked up about what happened about Dani going into that room, they'd have a long day ahead of them.

He was going to need more caffeine.

FROWNING AT THE NEWS PROGRAM, Louis muted the T.V.

A vibrating sound from his desk alerted him to a call. Snatching the phone from the drawer, he answered. "Who's this?"

"Actually, I'm a friend of Carver."

Louis huffed. "He's dead. How'd you get this number?"

"I have his phone. I wanted to have a chat with you regarding a situation Carver was working on. I think I can help."

Choosing his words carefully, Louis leaned back in his chair. "Oh? And what situation was Carver working on?"

"Well, I don't really want to discuss it on the phone."

"I'm not meeting you in person if that's what you're implying."

Silence stretched a moment as Louis took a sip of his morning OJ.

"Carver said he would mention me. That I could be of help."

The guy didn't sound like a cop, but no sense in taking chances.

"If you think you can help, I better see results. Quickly. You have two days. If you get my attention, then we can find a way to work together."

"Interesting terms. I'll see what I can do."

The call ended and Louis shoved the phone back inside the drawer. Glancing at the T.V., he turned up the sound.

"Dr. Shelby Durning was the victim of the assault by the now deceased attacker. But according to hospital administration, she's resting at home and in good condition."

A picture flashed across the screen. "Dierks Carver, a resident of the Rockwall community, was pronounced dead on scene after a tense stand-off with the TRT, the Tactical Response Team. You might recognize their name as the private SWAT team ready to take on special duties in order to keep east Dallas safe."

Louis frowned. Media affirmatives weren't what he wanted. The TRT needed to disappear before his chance at the mayoral election vanished. But the real question was why Carver was even at the hospital in the first place. And who was that doctor?

Mulling the death of his right-hand man, Louis had to find another reliable person that would carry out his deeds. Going through his normal channels would require owing even more to the new people he was working with, but he needed to know exactly who this man was with Carver's phone and whether or not he could be trusted.

There was too much to lose if he couldn't control this new contact. If this man proved reliable, perhaps he'd finally be done with the TRT, and his end of the bargain would be complete.

Pulling his phone from the desk, he placed a call. "We need to talk."

9

S helby rotated her head, releasing a pop, but the throbbing wouldn't stop.

She'd gone to the grocery store after a late breakfast, and now the coffee was wearing off. All she wanted was a nap, but her routine was too important. Since being active and doing her exercises was out of the question, there had to be another alternative that could help keep her eyes open.

Her phone went off and she jumped from the barstool to get to her purse. Groaning at the mistake of moving so quickly, she dug through the bag until her fingers felt the vibrating screen.

"Hello?"

"Dr. Durning?"

"Yes. Who's this?"

"I'm a reporter for the Dallas Post. I had a few questions."

Her jaw clenched. "I don't have anything to say about what happened."

"Oh, I'm not calling about that. I've been given some information about a previous crime involving you and a ring of counterfeiters."

"What?"

"Aren't you the same doctor that was accused of writing pads and pads of counterfeit narcotic prescriptions to sell on the street? How are you able to work here in Texas with that kind of record?"

"I think you have your information confused."

"No, I'm following up on a tip. According to my research, my information is correct."

"Get your facts straight, or you'll find yourself on the receiving end of a defamation lawsuit. Everything that happened is available to the public. I suggest you access it," she gritted out before hanging up the phone.

Informed by a tip? What tip? Who would call in a tip?

Pacing the living room, she gripped her phone to her chest. The memories flashed through her mind as her heart pounded. The hospital she had worked at when everything happened didn't renew her contract, and she ended up jobless. Because of the media storm that surrounded the situation, no one else in the area would hire her either.

Putting out resumes to anyone looking for a resident doctor, the hospital here had called, more than willing to take her on as soon as possible. After two years and moving to a different state, her reputation was finally building back up.

Swallowing the need to wallow, she grabbed a bottle of water from the fridge. Things were going well here. After all, just last week, she signed the paperwork to start part-time at a clinic. It could become a full-time job once her hospital contract was up.

She chewed on the inside of her cheek. But what if the reporter got it all wrong? What if a story was printed about what happened, and everyone started to think twice about her judgment? Or her abilities as a doctor?

Laying on the couch, she turned on the T.V. and stared at the screen, her fears and worries floating to the surface over the reporter and the next big story. If her colleagues found out, it would be another fiasco and everyone would scatter. It'd already happened once. Her family, friends, even co-workers had all left her standing, embarrassed and humiliated.

The clinic job, even the job at the hospital, could all be gone in a moment.

And if Jeff found out too? Even though they'd yet to even have a date, he seemed like the kind of guy that she could trust, maybe ...

Holding back a sob, she ignored the tears streaming down her face.

"I can't possibly make it through all this again," she whispered.

"THANKS FOR SPEAKING WITH ME. If I find anything else out, I'll let you know." Jeff frowned as he hung up with Randal's sister. After getting very little information from Detective Fredricks, he was able to piece together some information about Randal Goodwin.

A former Army specialist, Randal had some rough seasons overseas and retired two years ago. Living with his sister for the past seven months, she said he had been suffering from depression and spent some time at the VA seeing a therapist.

"Find anything out?" Buck walked into the room and sat on the couch.

"Not much. Randal's sister did say he was struggling with depression but has no idea why he was at the ER. Especially since he spent a lot of time at the VA and those services would've been free."

Buck nodded. "Did the sister give you any insight as to who he was seeing and if he was talking to a therapist for his depression?"

"She said he refused pills. He heard too many bad things could happen, but she didn't know the name of the doctor." Jeff stood and stretched out with a yawn. "He apparently had a job interview next week. His sister couldn't believe he would put that at risk. He'd waited months for an interview."

"It's a good thing you went by."

"I keep thinking that. It escalated so fast. One minute I'm asking about the victim from the hit and run, and the next, a guy pulls a knife and tries to kill Randal."

Buck stood. "This case with the doc, we're not investigating it, got it? I'm still working through our contacts about the mess a few months ago, we don't need another one."

Jeff huffed. "I'm not making a mess. I just don't understand what happened. I mean, Randal needs help, not sitting in jail for defending himself. With the young girl in the middle of it all, I'm afraid Fredricks might push a harsher punishment."

"I need you to tread lightly. We're still in the doghouse with some of these officers after what happened with Burnett." Buck patted his shoulder. "Get some rest and I'll poke around, see if I can figure something out discreetly."

"Thanks."

"I figured you'd be more interested in asking out the doctor instead of focusing on Randal."

"Ha ha. Very funny."

Buck shrugged. "Wasn't making a joke. She's pretty, smart, and has a good head on her shoulders. Why aren't you asking her out?"

"It's complicated." Jeff raked his fingers through his hair. "I mean, after everything that happened and her injury—"

"Excuses. Haven't I taught you anything?"

"You mean the bachelor that doesn't date and all the things you've taught me about being alone?" Jeff winced as the words came from his mouth.

"There was a time I wanted more, Jeff. But now, I'm content with what I have. You and Dani, Kyra, the rest of the team, this is my family now. I'm not alone."

Jeff nodded.

"But you should still ask her out." Buck turned and headed for his office.

Jeff let out a sigh and trudged from the office to his room, collapsing on the bed. Buck was right, of course. It was important to be here with family. And Buck did have a past, one Jeff was certain was filled with love at some point but must've ended badly. Buck never mentioned it, just got that haze in his eyes as if he were remembering. It always made him sad.

Dr. Shelby Durning's face lit his mind and he smiled. After refraining from texting her all day, he'd talked himself out of contact for at least today. She would definitely need her rest after the chain of events from yesterday.

So how was he going to casually build up a conversation with her?

He chuckled. It would be an interesting challenge.

"GOOD GRIEF," Shelby mumbled as she threw the covers off her legs.

At almost one in the morning, she was still wide awake. With a grunt, she slid off the bed and walked barefoot to the kitchen.

Passing out after that reporter's phone call had taken a few hours out of her afternoon, and now she was paying for it. A chill hit her bare legs and she paused in the kitchen, staring at the door that led to the garage.

Giving it a push, she closed it completely, and the alarm box next to the door turned green. "I know I shut it before bed." She searched the room. Everything appeared in place—nothing moving, no one hiding behind the couch.

Staring down at the doorknob, she groaned and locked the door, then grabbed the baseball bat she had tucked away in the corner.

Her swing ready, she went room by room and turned on all the lights, looked in all the closets and under the beds. Nothing.

Trudging back through the house, she turned the lights off and rechecked the doors and alarm before heading back to her room.

As she sat on the edge of the bed, she held her head and let out a yawn. For the first time in two years, the fear of being caught up in something illegal slammed into her chest, barely letting her take a breath.

"I've been cleared and found innocent of all the charges. Nothing can possibly happen now."

Tucking herself into bed, she closed her eyes and tried to focus on Jeff Powers and his bright blue eyes. If he did in fact call her again and ask her out, she'd be more than happy to take him up on his offer for coffee.

Maybe the distraction of a handsome man would push all the anxiety of what could transpire and the fear of the attack out of her mind, at least for tonight.

"God, give me some grace, please."

<h1 style="text-align:center">10</h1>

Jeff stood inside the visitor's center of the county jail, waiting for his name to be called.

"Powers?"

He stood and headed to the holding cell, stepping inside and to the table. A rustling came from behind him and Randal was escorted inside.

"Do I know you?" Randal looked better, more alert.

"Kind of. Have a seat." Jeff motioned to the bench and they both sat down. "How're you feeling?"

Randal shrugged. "Tired. I'm not sleeping and ... who are you?"

"My name is Jeff Powers. I was at the ER the other day."

Randal sighed and leaned his head back. "I don't even remember being there."

"Look, I saw what happened, and although I don't condone you using a little girl as a way to keep everyone back, I did see you divert an attack. I'm trying to piece it all together."

"You and me both." Randal leaned his cuffed hands on the table. "I just remember getting a text. A buddy said he was at the

ER. I was upset, and my sister, I'm living with her right now, was at work. I don't like to drive so I walked. But honestly, I don't really remember getting there or what happened. Every now and then, I get a flash … " Randal trailed off, staring down at his hands.

"So a friend texted you?"

"Yeah. Myles Nuñez. I visit him often at the VA. No one will tell me if he's okay." Randal's tired eyes met his. "Do you know?"

"I can check for you. Do you remember anything about the man that attacked you?"

"I told you, it's all a blur. Every now and then I get a memory about a man and I was holding on to someone. That's when the cops told me what happened. I should be in here. If I had hurt that girl, I'd never forgive myself." Randal sighed. "Just tell my sister I'm sorry. She won't take my calls."

"Have you talked to a lawyer?"

"Yeah, some guy right out of school. Not sure I've got a good chance." Randal managed a sad smirk. "But then again, maybe it's safer if I'm here."

Jeff shook his head. "Randal, what you did was wrong. But I do think there's something else going on here. Why would someone try and kill you?"

Randal shrugged. "Cops keep asking me the same thing. I have no idea."

"And you don't know Terry Quarters?"

"Never heard of him."

"Times up. Let's go."

Randal stood. "I'd appreciate it if you could see if Myles is okay."

"I'll see what I can do."

Jeff left the center, even more irritated. Either Randal was an exceptional liar, or he had blacked out on the way to the hospital. It could easily be PTSD, and once he was in fear for his buddy, it triggered a reaction.

Sliding into the SUV, he did a search on Myles Nuñez.

Something was nagging in his mind about all this, and he wasn't exactly sure why. He didn't know anyone involved, but so far, his team had been in the middle of two different situations regarding this man. One almost cost Dr. Durning her life, and that wasn't acceptable.

Not getting any hits, he headed back to the office to see if Buck could help him out.

"Sure, I'd love to pick up a few days this week." Shelby smiled into the phone, feeling lighthearted for the first time since the incident. "I do have to work at the hospital tomorrow, but I can pick up Friday or through this weekend?"

"Thanks so much. I'm really pushing for you to get more days, we really need another physician, and with your experience, I know you'd be an asset."

"Thanks, Marla. I really appreciate it."

"I'll send my schedule to you, okay?"

"Sounds great."

Shelby hung up with a sigh. Although she'd signed a conditional contract, the job wasn't hers yet. Waiting until the hospital contract came up was the next step, then she could sign on full time.

"Thanks, God," she whispered, her mind spinning.

At the computer, she scrolled through the emails until Marla's came into view. As she read, her phone buzzed.

"Hello?"

"Dr. Durning?"

"Yes?"

"This is Detective Fredricks. I need you to come down to the station and go over a few things and sign a statement. Would you have time today to do that?"

"Of course. When do I need to show up?"

"Just whenever you get a chance to sit down with us."

"Okay, I'll be there in an hour or so."

"Sounds good."

The call ended and Shelby leaned back in her chair. Going over everything again, reliving that scene in the hospital ... a shiver rushed through her body. It was a nightmare that didn't seem to want to end.

Touching her throat, she eased her fingers over the bruises. The skin was only damaged on one side, but her entire neck was sore. Swallowing hard, she stood and went to check her stitches and make a run to town.

11

"Myles Nuñez?" Jeff frowned as the line went dead. "No luck?"

He looked up at Buck. "I'm pretty sure that was the right one."

"You get the number from Randal's sister?"

"Yeah, she let me look at an old address book Randal had on his dresser. I tried to explain what was going on, but since I don't really know, I don't think I helped things."

Buck sat down across from him in the office. "Look, we can't fix everything. You know that."

Jeff leaned back. "I know. But this guy, I can't see him as starting anything. By the time I turned around, it looked like he was trying to stop Terry Quarters from attacking him."

"And you think Myles can give you answers?"

"I think Myles can tell me why Randal was at the ER that morning."

Buck sighed and reached across the desk, grabbing a file. "I had a buddy of mine take a look into Myles." He tossed the file to Jeff. "Guys got some issues, been in and out of jail, can't hold a job."

"Is this his address?"

Buck shrugged. "Last known. You can check it out, but tread lightly."

"Thanks." Jeff jumped from the seat and headed to his room to grab his gear.

"What's up?" Danica leaned on the doorframe.

"Wanna take a trip?"

"This to see the doctor?"

"No. I'm going to see a friend of Randal's. They spoke the day of the incident and told Randal to meet at the ER."

"Sure. Haiden's at the range."

"Let's go." Jeff stepped into the garage and loaded his gear into the back of the SUV, just in case it was needed.

Evan pulled into the other side of the garage and emerged from his truck. Jeff opened the driver's side door. "You busy?"

"Not at the moment. You got plans?"

"Might need some backup if you're interested."

"You've got Danica."

Jeff shrugged. "Might need someone like you there."

Evan narrowed his eyes and gave a nod.

Parked down the block from Myles Nuñez's address, Jeff studied the area.

"So, we don't know for certain if this is *the* Myles, right?" Evan's deep voice rumbled from the back seat.

"Trust me, it's him."

"Jeff and I can approach. Evan, you want to sit back and watch?" Danica turned in the seat.

Evan nodded. "I've got a spot picked out. Give me five to get in place, then you guys can make contact."

The door opened and slammed shut.

"Why did you bring Evan? I was hoping we could talk."

Jeff frowned. "I needed another set of eyes on the house in case Myles gets defensive."

"Okay, so let's talk now."

Ignoring the invite, he opened the door and slid to the curb.

"It's not been five minutes."

"It's close enough. Besides, the longer we sit in that SUV, the longer Myles has to form a plan."

"We're over a block away. I doubt he noticed us."

"Our SUV in this area, I'm sure we've been spotted." Jeff studied the leaning chain-link fence as they walked past.

The neighborhood needed some work. It was an older part of town and the houses showed their age. Overgrown yards and trees lined the sidewalks, spilling out and over the edge with dried-up leaves that rattled in the wind.

Jeff nudged Danica across the street and they took the steps to the front door.

"Good cop, bad cop?"

"We're not cops," he muttered as he knocked on the door.

The door finally cracked open.

"Yeah?"

"My name's Jeff. I'm a friend of Randal's. Can we talk?"

"I don't talk to cops."

"We're not cops." Danica stepped forward. "We're just worried about Randal and hoped you could help us."

Jeff stepped back as Myles opened the door wider, studying Danica up and down.

"Guess you're not cops. What do *you* need, pretty lady?"

"Randal said he spoke to you two days ago. That you're why he was at the ER?"

Myles frowned and searched the area a moment before finally stepping through the door. "Look, I was there. But I guess Randal beat me because when I showed, cops were everywhere and no one was getting in. I came back here and decided to wait him out."

"Are you okay?"

Myles nodded at Jeff. "Better today. Randal told you?"

"He told me you had headaches."

Myles shifted, studying Jeff. "Yeah, bad. I was real sick, couldn't drive, so I had to walk. All the lights from the cars at the ER, it was making it worse. I came back home and closed the curtains and was able to sleep it off."

Jeff clamped his mouth shut. Myles seemed much more interested in talking to Danica.

"Has Randal been feeling okay?"

Myles shrugged. "Like how?"

"His sister mentioned he was depressed," Jeff answered.

"Not anymore than the rest of us."

"Myles, can I ask a sensitive question?" Danica gently pressed a hand on Myles' arm. "Has Randal ever blacked out before?"

"Yeah, a couple of times." Myles backed up and leaned against the house. "He's my best friend, a good guy. He'd do anything for you. But he still reacts sometimes. We all do it when we come back. A car backfires or fireworks, we all hit the deck. Randal just can't shake it. If he sees someone watching him, he gets nervous.

"He's never acted on it, not unless whoever was watching started it. But a few months back, some guy cornered him outside this little mom-and-pop grocery store. I think the guy tried to hold him up." Myles chuckled. "I heard a yell and a gunshot. I rushed around the corner and Randal had the gun in pieces, the guy on the ground yelling that his arm was broken."

"Did the police get involved?" Jeff crossed his arms.

Myles shook his head. "I took the gun, wiped it down, and threw the pieces in the dumpster. We took off. Randal didn't even remember what happened by the time we got home."

"Sounds like he took care of business."

Myles straightened at the sound of Evan's voice, his eyes narrowing as he stared past Jeff. "Yeah."

"Have you heard the name Terry Quarters?"

Myles shook his head at Jeff, his gaze cutting behind him to Evan.

Jeff pulled up a picture of Terry on his phone. "What about this man?"

Miles frowned. "Guy's a jerk."

"So you recognize him?" Danica asked.

"Sure. He goes by Payday. Some guy Randal knows from way back."

"How do you know him?"

Miles glowered at Evan. "Met him a few times. Always in trouble or looking for it. Not someone I hang out with."

"I was told he only has a few charges in the past, nothing significant."

"Then he's not been caught yet. If he's involved with whatever is going on with Randal, then I don't want to be."

"Jeff." Evan nodded to the side.

"Thanks for talking to us." Danica smiled and shook Miles' hand.

"Tell Randal I'll keep an eye on his sister. I'll get him whatever he needs. I just can't get involved if there's something else going down. I've got two strikes. One more and I go away for a long time. That's not going to happen."

"I think he understands." Jeff took his card from his wallet. "Call me if you need anything. Not just what's going on with Randal."

Myles took the card with a nod.

Back on the street, Jeff paused as Evan stopped in front of him. "What've you got?"

"Based on what I've heard, I think Randal was doing what he could to not only protect himself but to protect the one person that would need it the most."

"A little girl."

Jeff nodded at Danica. "But he wouldn't let her go. I asked several times."

"Doesn't matter. Once that switch is flipped, he's in protection mode and isn't concerned about anything else. If Terry Quarters is that dangerous, once Randal saw the knife, he would want to protect everyone around him. Randal would go on defense."

"Do you think Randal knows him?" Danica questioned.

"Randal might not even remember that his real name is Terry or might not know." Evan shrugged. "A lot of guys have nicknames in the military and they stick even once you get out."

Jeff blew out a deep breath. "Let's get back. I'll see if I can talk to Randal again, bring up the name Payday and a picture."

"Don't get your hopes up on this one, Jeff. It's going to be hard to prove that Randal was trying to protect that girl."

Jeff nodded at Evan's comment as they climbed into the SUV. Either way it fell, he wasn't going to just leave Randal in prison with no answers and no one to turn to.

12

"Can I help you?"

Shelby gave a nod to the officer.

"Yes, Detective Fredricks asked me to meet him here. He said he had some questions."

"Your name?"

"Shelby Durning."

"Have a seat." The officer motioned to the waiting area.

Legs bouncing, she tried to ease her breathing. After giving statements to everyone after both incidents, it didn't make sense that she'd need to be here now. Maybe the detective found out why the man was in the ER and why the other man tried to kill her.

Lord, calm my nerves.

"Ms. Durning?"

She stood.

"I'm Detective Fredricks. Can you come with me?"

Gripping her purse in front of her, she followed the detective to the desk and sat down in the offered chair.

"Can I get you anything?"

"Um, no. What is it you needed?"

"We just had some questions."

A familiar face sat down next to the detective.

"You remember Detective Alson from the hospital?"

She nodded.

"How're you feeling? I was told you were injured."

"There's a cut on my back from the man that had the knife. It's been stitched up. I'm just a little sore."

Detective Fredricks nodded. "Do you recognize the name Ryan Cushing?"

Her jaw tensed as her heartbeat quickened. "Of course. You have the reports, you know the situation."

"Have you spoken to him recently?"

"No. I've had no contact in three years with anyone involved. Why would you even ask?"

"We just want to be sure we've covered all our bases."

Her shoulders tensed. "All bases? Tell me, detective, why was Terry Quarters in the ER that morning? And why was that man trying to kill him and me? How could any of this possibly have anything to do with Ryan?"

"Glad you asked." Detective Fredricks pulled a picture from his folder and handed it to her. "Terry Quarters asked for you specifically."

She declined to take the picture. "I have no idea who he is."

The detective sat the picture down in front of her. "He had your card in his apartment."

"Good for him. I give my card to all my patients, and it's available at the front desk in the hospital and at the clinic I work at. Anyone can grab one. I've never met him. You get a warrant to circumvent HIPAA and you can check my files. He's not my patient."

"Just as you said, per HIPAA, you're not allowed to tell us about your relationship."

"I'm not. But I am allowed to tell you he's not my patient." She glared between the two men. "Have you checked to see if he's been to the clinic? There are five other doctors there currently. He could be a patient of theirs."

"I'll see if we can find a friendly judge, but you do know how difficult it is to get around HIPAA regulations. The man isn't deceased, just unconscious."

"You have my permission to check anything you want of mine. I have no idea who Terry Quarters is or how he got my number. I also have no idea who the man was that tried to kill Terry."

"Dierks Carver."

"What?"

"His name was Dierks Carver." The detective took out another picture. "Do you recognize the name?"

"No. I don't know who he is either," she mumbled, swallowing bile burning the back of her throat from looking at the man in the picture.

"Dr. Durning, I'm just asking these questions because the incident happened in the ER where you work, then again to you in the hospital. All the clues seem to be pointing to you."

"You can follow the clues wherever they lead, it won't be to me. I was hoping you'd have answers, something to tell me why this all happened at the hospital and why it happened to me."

Detective Fredricks frowned. "Dr. Durning, I know it's hard for you to see this, but the fact is, Terry Quarters asked to see you that morning, and then, according to your statement at the hospital, Dierks Carver attempted to kill him. Why do you think Mr. Carver was looking so hard to find Mr. Quarters?"

She shrugged as her face heated. "I don't know. It's not like we had a friendly conversation in the hospital room. I was doing everything I could to keep Mr. Quarters alive and that other man was determined to either wake him or kill him. He never told me why." Gripping her purse, she stood. "If you really think I'm behind any of this, you can check my phone records, email, everything. I've had no contact with Mr. Quarters, the man that tried to kill him, or Ryan."

"Sounds good. Follow me, please."

How could they think she had anything to do with what

happened? She was found innocent of all charges almost three years ago and had worked non-stop to get her career back on track.

"If you can just sign these forms, it'll give us authorization to check all your phone records."

God, please give me a break here.

STRIDING THROUGH THE DOUBLE DOORS, Jeff headed toward Detective Fredricks' desk. Pausing, he smiled. Shelby was leaning over a desk, working on some forms.

He stood to the side to wait. Although he wanted to discuss the connection of Terry and Randal to Fredricks, he'd much rather have a conversation with Shelby. Dressed in leggings and a long purple sweater, he grinned as she turned and headed for the door.

"Oh, hi Jeff." She offered a small smile as her cheeks reddened.

"Hey. What're you doing here?"

She slid on her coat with a grimace. "I had to speak to someone. What're you doing?"

"I was going to talk to someone too, but now I'd rather go for coffee. There's a small café around the corner. Would you like to join me?"

Her eyes went wide. "Um, okay. I've never turned down coffee."

"Good to know." He grinned and ushered her out the door and into the brisk breeze. "It's a little chilly to walk, how about I drive?"

That blank stare hit him again. "Sure," she mumbled as she zipped up her coat.

Taking her elbow, he led her to his truck and opened the door for her to slide in. Once behind the wheel, he turned the heat all the way up.

"You doing all right?"

Silence stretched.

"Shelby?" He turned to see her push her hair back.

"Sorry, I'm a bit distracted. I've not had much sleep."

"No need to apologize. It's been a rough few days."

Hearing her sigh, he frowned at the once smiling and friendly doctor suffering from the tragedies of the last time he saw her. After he parked, he rushed around and huffed as she slid from the seat, slamming the door.

"What's wrong?"

"I was coming to open the door for you."

A sliver of a smile came out and he grinned. "Thanks. You're quite the gentleman."

"You're quite welcome." He opened the coffee shop door with a flourish, and she let out a chuckle.

After ordering large coffees and a few muffins, they slid into a small booth at the back of the shop.

Jeff shucked his jacket in the warm building, and Shelby did the same. The purple sweater hung loosely over her shoulders and he struggled to bring his eyes to hers.

"So, how long have you worked with Buck and the others?"

"Well, the TRT has only been around a few years. Buck brought me on the second the funding appeared and we've been building ever since."

"You do good work. I've heard of you."

"Oh? I'm glad it's good. Here lately, we've had some bad press."

She nodded along, cupping her chin in her hand as she stirred creamer into her coffee.

"Shelby, how're you doing? Really?"

She paused and straightened. "Is there any way we can talk about something else? Honestly, I'd like to forget about the whole thing."

He reached out and took hold of her hand before he could think. "I can understand being tired and wanting to forget. But the best way to get over something like this is to talk to someone."

"It's not that easy," she whispered. "I have my job and reputation to think of."

"I know of a few people I would trust completely to be discreet. I'll send you those numbers."

She nodded, her gaze focused on his hand. It was then he realized she hadn't even tried to hold his hand back.

Relenting his grip, he took hold of his mug. Silence stretched as she sipped at her coffee.

"Tell me, what made you want to become a doctor? That's a pretty big ambition."

A real smile seeped through and his heart jumped.

"I've always enjoyed helping people, it just came naturally. My mother was a nurturer and I just ..." she sighed. "School almost made me want to quit. It's not an easy task."

"I imagine not. Did you always want to work at a hospital?"

"Not specifically. I really wanted to work overseas, doctors without borders kind of thing. But that never, um, it didn't work out." She took a long sip of her coffee.

"How long have you been here in Dallas? I detect a bit of a southern accent."

She let out a chuckle. "I'm from Arkansas."

"Oh, one of those Razorback fanatics."

"You better believe it." She gave him a wink.

"So you moved all the way out here instead of staying there?"

Her eyes jutted past his. "Oh, well, I've been a few places. This is hopefully the last move I make. I'm looking to get established enough to work for a clinic."

"Why the change?"

Her eyebrow perked. "Why all the questions?"

He shrugged. "Just getting to know you. So far, every time we're together, it's all very rushed."

A smile curled on her bright red lips. "Working at the hospital is very rewarding. I've done it most of my career. But it's demanding and with family so far away, I'd like to move into a position that would allow me some time off when I need it."

"I can understand that."

"You have family far away?"

"No, not much family left, actually. Buck and Danica, they're my family."

Her eyes dropped. "Sorry about that."

"Don't be."

As she picked at the small muffin in front of her, all the chaos and drama that surrounded her suddenly hit him. The far away, distracted looks, the sadness in her voice, she'd suffered a lot in the last few days. Maybe he could be the one to give her a break.

"As much as I would like to sit here and ask more questions, I do have to get back to the police station to give the detective some information. But maybe we can finish this conversation tonight over dinner?"

She straightened, her hands falling to her lap. "Oh. I guess, that sounds good."

"Shelby." He leaned forward and tapped the table in front of her. "If you don't want to go, you don't have to say yes."

"Why would you say that?"

"I can tell you're unsure."

She frowned. "Former Homeland with extensive police background, are you profiling me?"

He grinned that she remembered all that. "I don't have to profile to tell that you're hesitant."

"Not unsure, just careful. Women these days have to be careful. Don't you agree?"

"Of course. But you don't need to feel obligated just because I helped to save your life."

Her jaw dropped then a big smile replaced it. "Just so you know, I'm not saying yes because I feel obligated."

"Good." He stood and slid from the booth, pulling his jacket on.

"Is that what you intended? To guilt me into going?" She stood.

He chuckled and helped her into the coat, leaning to her ear. "Of course not. You'd already said yes," he whispered.

The slight shiver that moved through her body made his smile that much wider as he placed a hand on her back to lead her out of the café. He once more opened the door to his truck for her and then slid behind the wheel.

"You, Dr. Durning, are an interesting woman."

"Interesting? What does that mean?"

He smiled at her narrowed gaze studying him from the other seat. "It means I'd like to get to know more about you."

She huffed. "Do you always say what's on your mind?"

"Nope." He stopped at the light. "I learned a long time ago to keep my mouth shut. It tends to get me into trouble. But I will say I've been holding back quite a bit lately."

Her cheeks reddened as she smiled and looked away.

That smile, he could get used to seeing it every day.

"The light's green, Jeff."

Forcing his gaze to the road, he headed back to the police station and parked next to her car.

Ushering her from his car to hers, he waited outside her door as she started it up and rolled the window down. Her gaze flicked to his, studying his face once more. Forcing his hands to stay firmly in his pockets, he resisted the urge to reach out as he leaned into the door.

"So, you're going to call me later?"

"Yes, any preferences?"

"I'm not that picky."

He huffed. "I doubt that."

"Not about food." She chuckled. "Just tell me where we're going so I know what to wear."

"Is that code for someplace fancy?"

"No, no code. I've not been to very many places around here, surprise me."

"You like surprises?"

Her eyes narrowed. "No, actually, I don't. But this is just dinner. I can do dinner."

He smiled at her candor, his focus once more on her lips.

"I'll see you later, Jeff."

His eyes bounced to hers. "I'll give you a call."

With that, she backed out of the lot as he stood there staring.

"God, what kind of plan do you have here?" he mumbled.

Shelby was an amazing woman with layers to her personality and her past. Tonight was going to have to be special, and his heart pounded at the thought.

It was going to be a long afternoon.

***

"Wow," Shelby mumbled as she pulled into traffic and headed home.

Jeff was so easy to talk to and funny and ... this was too soon to feel all overcome after a coffee date. But after the last, well, three years, finding someone to date wasn't just hard, it was impossible.

Not that it was all the guy's fault. With her past, she was over-protective and kept her guard up. So much so that the few dates she had been on told her it was obvious she wasn't interested and they'd moved on. Except she had been interested, just careful. And scared. And terrified they'd do something to ruin or hurt her. "You're such a mess," she mumbled, turning down the street to her house.

It was bad enough she kept away from men in general, but now, a great guy who was obviously trustworthy wanted to take her out, and she was terrified.

Pulling into her driveway, she froze at the sight of her garage door wide open.

"I ... I know I shut it before I left," she whispered.

Shoving the car in park, she stared at the open door and called Jeff's number without even thinking.

"Powers."

"Um, Jeff?"

"Hey, Shelby. Everything okay?"

"No, I mean, I'm not sure. My garage door is open."

"You're certain you closed it?"

"Of course."

"Let me come check the house, just in case."

Her face heating, she swallowed hard. "Thanks, Jeff."

13

Jeff pulled up to Shelby's house and parked on the road. Jogging to her door, he knocked on the window. "Hey. You okay?"

A trembling lip and the way she clutched her phone to her chest told him no.

"Roll down the window, please." Shoving his hands in his pockets, he waited until she did so. "Shelby? Did something else happen? Did you see someone?"

"It's probably nothing and I ..." she trailed off.

"Tell me what's happened. From the beginning."

Her eyes jumped from him to the house. "Last night, I know I closed the doors and locked them. I mean, I always do. But the door to the garage was slightly ajar. I went through the house, but there was no one there and my alarm never went off. Now this."

Pulling his phone, he dialed Buck. "Wait in the car. Lock the doors just in case, okay?" He stepped away, hand on his weapon.

"Thompson."

"I'm just giving you a heads up. I'm at Shelby's house, and there's something going on here."

"Define something."

"Her door was open last night after she remembers closing and locking it. She came home and the garage door is open."

"You don't think she's forgetting?"

"Normally, I would jump to that conclusion. But she's a doctor, repetition is one of their personality traits."

"On my way."

"I'm going to clear it."

"Copy."

Hanging up, Jeff entered the garage, studying the sensors to make sure nothing had obscured them from closing when she left this morning. Finding it clear, he used his shirt to twist the knob, easing the door open.

The smell of gas flooded his senses and he dashed from the house.

"Back up, Shelby. Now!"

Putting in a call to the gas company, he took several breaths of clean air.

"National Gas Services."

"I need you to shut off the gas to 1783 Los Rancho Ave. There's a possible gas leak."

"Let me get my supervisor."

"There's no time, shut it off! I can't get in there safely to do it."

"I have to get permission."

The call clicked over and Jeff jogged up to Shelby and knocked on her window. "Move down farther, get away from the house. There's a gas leak."

"What?"

"Shelby, just do it. Please."

With wide eyes, she backed farther down as Buck passed and parked in the road.

"What's the word?"

"Gas leak. I'm trying to get them to turn it off."

"Let me have that. You go speak to the doctor."

Handing over the phone, Jeff made his way to Shelby. Tears running down her flushed cheeks, she stared blankly at the house.

"Shelby? Look at me." After knocking several times on the window, he grabbed the handle and sighed. "Unlock the door, please."

She fumbled with the keys in her hand and then hit the button on the door. Stepping in close, he took her hand.

"Shelby? What's going on here?"

"I don't know," she whispered.

The reaction, her fear, it could all just be from the attacks and lack of sleep. "Is there anything else you want to talk about?"

She shook her head.

"We'll get it taken care of, okay?"

"I ... I'm sorry I called. I should've just called the police. I'm sure you have more important things to do," she mumbled.

"I'd rather help you out than spend my day at the range running drills." He let out a chuckle that she ignored.

"They've got it turned off, but they're sending a crew to investigate. Police are on their way too." Buck handed him the phone. "Shelby, do you know what's going on?"

"No, I have no idea."

"I'm going to make sure there's nothing leaking in the houses next door." Buck glanced at Jeff before heading to the next house.

"I don't even use my stove and my water heater is ... I think it's electric?"

"It could be a leak, it could be lots of things. Let's not jump until we know exactly what's going on, okay?"

Chewing on her lip, she wiped the back of her hand over her cheeks. Judging from her tired eyes staring at the house, the most logical explanation was that she forgot to shut her door last night and now the garage door.

But then again, someone as guarded as Shelby wouldn't just forget to close her door. Not when he could barely get her to agree to coffee. She was careful, meticulous, and safety-conscious.

So who would be able to get past her vigilant nature, and what could she have done to make them so vengeful?

14

Shelby waited impatiently for the police detective to finally make his way to her.

It was a nightmare coming true. Someone was haunting her. The first person that came to mind was still in jail, right? With the detective already questioning her about Ryan, he would've mentioned if Ryan was out of jail. Wouldn't he?

"Dr. Durning?"

She stood from the front bumper of her car.

"Let's talk over here."

Following Detective Fredricks with a frown, she could feel Jeff's eyes watching as they made it to the detective's car.

"So, Mr. Powers mentioned your door being open last night too?"

"Yes. I couldn't sleep so I got up and went to the kitchen. That's when I noticed the door to the garage slightly open. I always close and lock everything up and set my alarm before I go to bed."

"You don't think you could've forgotten?"

Her jaw clenched as she crossed her arms. "No. I didn't forget. Why would you assume?"

"The gas on your stove was left on. Two burners were turned

all the way to high. Another few hours and the whole house would've exploded with just a spark."

"I don't even cook in the mornings. I had some coffee and a power bar before I left. There's no reason for me to even use the stove."

Detective Fredricks looked less than amused. "Dr. Durning, I know you've had a few rough days—"

She stepped into his space. "I'm no longer entertaining this line of questions. I didn't forget, and I sure didn't leave the gas on in my own home. I just told you I don't even use the stove in the mornings."

"Is there a problem?"

Ignoring Jeff's voice from behind, she stepped back. "I'll be in my car."

"Shelby? Hey, wait up."

Sliding into her car, she started it and turned to Jeff as he stood in her door. "I'm sorry I called. I shouldn't have bothered you."

"No bother. I'm glad I could help." His eyes narrowed. "You have no idea what's going on? No angered patients or anything?"

"I've not even been here long enough for anyone to be angered." She let out a sigh. "I'm sorry. This is all ... it's a lot. I appreciate you coming when you did."

"Mind if I take a look inside?"

Her gaze jumped to his. "Why?"

He shrugged. "If someone was there, I want to see if I can figure out why."

"You don't think I just forgot?"

He chuckled. "Shelby, although I don't know you all that well, you don't strike me as the type to simply let things slip your mind. Especially anything that would make you safe."

Chewing on the inside of her cheek, she nodded. "Okay, but just a quick look, right? I mean, I can trust you not to snoop, can't I?"

As he gave a grin, her bluetooth went off.

"Durning."

"Shelby? Is everything okay?"

She sighed at Dr. Allison's voice over the line. Taking the phone off speaker, she covered it a moment and looked at Jeff. "Can you give me a second?"

He nodded and stepped back.

"Dr. Allison, do you need me to come in?"

"Is everything all right? An officer was at the hospital and asked if you worked here, said there was an emergency."

"There was a gas leak and I had to call the police to shut everything off. But I'm fine. I'll be in tomorrow morning."

"Well, if you think that's the best idea."

Closing her eyes, Shelby fought back tears. "Of course, I'll be fine."

"If you need to take some more time—"

"Dr. Allison, I appreciate you checking on me. But really, this was just one of those things, and because of the gas, the police had to become involved. I'm sure it'll be resolved soon. I'll see you in the morning."

"I'm glad it's all settled. Take care."

The call ended and she leaned against the steering wheel.

Lord, what am I going to do? Everyone thinks I'm completely inept or simply forgetful.

Straining to remember, the memory jumped out. This morning, as she backed from the drive, she hit the button and waited for the door to shut before driving away.

So if she was the one who closed it, who could've opened it?

JEFF WATCHED as Shelby held her head. Her amber eyes stared at the house, her fingers still wiping at the dried tears on her cheeks.

"She okay?"

He shrugged at Buck. "Not sure."

"You think she forgot?"

"Nope."

Buck turned with a frown.

"Look, she's a meticulous woman. I've seen the inside of her home. If it were just the garage or the door, then maybe. But both? One at night and one in the morning? What does that sound like to you?"

"Someone got inside and then wanted out."

"Exactly." Jeff's gaze went to Shelby. "And they wanted her to notice."

She slid from the SUV and slammed the door closed. As she walked his way, the car beeped.

"Everything all right?"

"My boss heard about what was going on and wanted to check up. I guess I can let you walk through since I'll be going in to gather up some things. Is it safe yet?"

"They opened up the windows and doors and shut everything off. You planning on staying somewhere?"

"Might as well."

Following her inside, he stopped to study the door. "It was this door that was open?"

"Yes, just a crack. But the alarm would've told me if the door was open."

He nodded. The lock appeared untouched, the door without marks from tampering.

"What is it you want to look for?"

Straightening, he glanced around the room. "Just wanted to see if I could find anything out of place."

"But wouldn't I be better suited to find something out of place? It is *my* house."

He chuckled. "Yes. You look around and let me know if you find anything that looks moved or adjusted."

Glancing over his shoulder, he smiled at her furrowed eyebrows as she surveyed the room.

"The lamp. It's not in the right spot."

He followed her gaze and looked it over. The ring on the carpet was clear it had shifted a few inches. "Great catch," he mumbled as he pulled on a pair of latex gloves.

"You keep gloves with you?"

"Only if I'm on a scene." Tipping the tall lamp, he felt the base and then looked up into the shade. A small black dot appeared. "Can you go get Buck for me?"

"Why?"

He stood, sweeping his hand over the bug and pulling it from the shade. "I need him to help me look for more of these."

15

After an hour of searching, Jeff had a major headache from the fumes as well as ten small listening devices from Shelby's home. Standing on the porch with Detective Fredricks, he waited for the judgment.

"I'll have to see if the techs can ID these for me."

"Will you let me know?"

"Not sure that's in your purview," Fredricks answered.

"Okay, what about surveillance?"

"From whom?"

"Whoever planted those bugs."

Fredricks glanced at the commotion of officers on the front lawn. "Mr. Powers, I can appreciate what you're trying to do here. But Dr. Durning is staying elsewhere, so there's no reason to keep watch. Whoever planted these has noticed police at the house for hours now and is long gone. He's not coming back to collect."

"You can't say that for certain. He might try and cover his tracks. What about protective custody for Shelby?"

"She doesn't want it. I already asked if she would like for us to send a unit by wherever she decides to stay."

Jeff clamped his mouth shut.

"Mr. Powers, I'd appreciate it if you could keep this information to yourself. I don't want to read about it in the paper tomorrow."

"I know how to do my job, Detective. I'd never risk giving out information on an active case."

Fredricks frowned. "I've heard of all of you, the TRT. You've had some bad situations recently and have issues keeping your people in check."

"As do you."

That got him a glare.

"Let's just agree that this is a police investigation. I've already informed Dr. Durning to keep pertinent details to herself as well. That includes from you too."

"And Randal? What about the information I gave you?"

Fredricks turned. "That's a need-to-know situation. Once I speak with him, I'll see if I can share that information."

Jeff watched as the detective walked away.

"Good job," Buck mumbled from behind him.

"He's lucky I didn't point out his inept attitude."

"Jeff, I told you, this can't become some issue we have to try and solve. You need to drop both Randal's case as well as this one."

Jeff turned to Buck. "Seriously? The woman had her home broken into and bugged while she slept."

"You can't make her do anything she doesn't want to do. If she doesn't want protection, that's her choice."

Jeff's hands fisted as Buck left. He was right. Shelby had the option to turn down help. But after what happened to her at the hospital, why would she?

Making his way to her car, she slammed the back and started to climb into the front seat.

"Shelby?"

She yanked the door shut and started the car, rolling down the window.

"Detective Fredricks told me you turned down protection?"

"I'm sorry I involved you. This is all such a mess." She chewed on her bottom lip a moment.

"I don't mind helping. After what happened the other day, I think you should consider allowing the police to set up protection."

Her eyes jutted to where the detectives stood. "Look, they already don't even like me, and now with all this and you—"

"Wait, why wouldn't they like you?"

"It's a long story and I'm just so tired." She pushed her hair back. "I guess from all the fumes."

He studied her for a moment. "If you need to call, call."

Her wide eyes searched everywhere ahead of her.

"Look at me, Shelby."

Her glassy eyes met his. It wasn't just uncertainty, it was fear she was holding on to.

"You can call me anytime you want to talk or even if you're just worried. Okay?"

"I appreciate that, Jeff." Once more, her gaze went to the detectives. "But it would probably be best if you find something else to focus on. I'm afraid I'm not going to be as free as I once was."

"What does that mean?"

She sighed and buckled her seat belt. "Whatever this is, I would hate for it to spill out onto you or the group you work with."

"It's our job to help people."

"I know, but I ..." her jaw clenched. "I'm not sure you know what you're getting into."

Stepping closer to the door, he leaned an elbow on the open window. "Shelby, is there something you're holding back? Do you know who's doing this?"

She shook her head, wiping a few tears from her cheeks. "No."

"Then what would I be getting into?"

She swallowed hard, his eyes staring at her long neck as the hair piled up on her head had already started to trail down.

"Shelby?"

"I've got to go." Clearing her throat, she gave him a forced smile. "Thanks for being so quick, again."

"Always."

With a nod, he stepped back as she rolled up the window and sped away. As he watched her disappear, he scanned the crowd of vans and reporters that had shown up for the story. A black sedan with tinted windows pulled from a side road, spinning out the back tires as it turned to follow Shelby's car.

"We need to get going. Don't say a word to anyone," Buck mumbled and pushed past him.

The reporters had surrounded the area, making it a pool of cameras and cell phones to wade through.

"What can you tell us?"

"Is this another attack on the TRT?"

"Was anyone injured?"

The reporters hung on his arms as he battled through the throng and to his truck. Slipping inside, it took another ten minutes before they could clear the crowd and leave the scene.

What's going on here? Why is she being targeted? Doors opened, the bugs in her home—what was she hiding that someone obviously wanted?

God, why did You lead me to her if she's going to keep me in the dark?

The irony of his prayer hit Jeff's stomach. He had things in his past he was holding back, but nothing that could possibly bring him harm. Ignoring the prod, he pushed away those thoughts as well.

What he was holding back could end up hurting her. So how was that so different from what she was doing?

16

Shelby sat on the edge of the bed in the hotel room, attempting to stifle more sobs. Someone was trying to destroy her, and she only knew of one person that would work so hard to make her miserable.

Pulling out her phone, she called Stephanie, the only friend she had left in Tampa.

"Shel?"

"Hey, Steph."

"I haven't heard from you in months! How's it going?"

Taking a deep breath, Shelby held in those ever present fears. "Well, things were actually going well. I thought I was on my way to a private practice."

"Sounds great! What happened?"

"I need to ask you something."

"Sure, anything."

"Have you heard if Ryan's out?"

Silence stretched.

"Steph?"

"Look, I've not heard a word about it. But if you're asking, that means something's happening."

"Some strange things that I don't understand. And someone gave a tip to a reporter about what happened and she called."

"Oh no, I'm so sorry. I've not heard anything about any of them, but I'm not exactly keeping tabs. They have a ten-year sentence, right?"

"Minimum," Shelby mumbled. "With everything going on, I just can't imagine who else it could possibly be."

"You're telling me you don't have any patients that are upset?"

Shelby scoffed. "I think you forget how good my bedside manner is." She grinned at Stephanie's laughter from the other end.

"Enough about the bad stuff. Tell me the good."

"Not much to tell," Shelby stood, just to ease into the bed once more, leaning against the headboard.

"You've not met any cute doctors there? That's hard to believe."

"No, no doctors."

"So there is someone? Spill."

Shelby grimaced. "No, just a friend. Well, I think he's a friend."

"So what's wrong with him?"

"Nothing."

"Then you need to be a friend to him."

Shelby chuckled. "I'll think about it."

"Good. I've got a lot going on. You're going to need an entire notebook to keep up with the insanity here."

As Stephanie rambled about the hospital they used to work at together, Shelby's mind wondered to Jeff and his questions. Of course she didn't have any idea who would do this to her. Bug her home? Really?

But if it wasn't Ryan putting her through all this, then who else could it be? Jeff did say he worked in several different law enforcement agencies, maybe he could find out if Ryan was still in jail? Just in case.

But then again, letting Jeff know about any of this, what would he think of her?

She had lost everyone else; family, friends who thought she was so foolish they were embarrassed to know her. Stephanie was the only one left.

If she lost Jeff too? Before they even had a chance?

Closing her eyes, she shook her head. It didn't matter now. She'd told him to back off and her world was crashing. Did she really want him there for that too?

JEFF PACED THE OFFICE, his mind running.

Even if Shelby didn't know exactly who had turned on the gas, she knew much more than what she gave him. He'd barely been able to get through the training this afternoon, and now his mind was on overdrive, attempting to piece together what was going on.

Maybe if he looked deeper ...

Shaking his head, he grabbed a bottle of water from the fridge. Looking up a past without permission was something you did when you were going after someone, not trying to help.

"Problems?" Danica sat down on the couch. "What's going on? You've got something on your mind."

"Something happened at Shelby's house."

"Oh?" she grinned.

"Not like that." Sitting on the recliner facing her, he leaned on his knees. "She found her door open last night, and then today her garage door was open."

"Did she forget?"

"No. The gas was left on and Buck and I found ten listening devices in her house."

Danica leaned forward. "What? Who would do that?"

"She said she doesn't know."

"Then what's the deal?"

He stood and paced.

"You don't believe her?"

"She's holding back. I think there's something in her past, something she doesn't want to talk about."

"Jeff. You've got to slow down here. You've not even gone on a date."

He wasn't able to hold back his grin.

"What?" She jumped up with a smile. "When did that happen?"

"This morning. We went for coffee and I asked her out tonight. But then all this happened and she said I shouldn't get involved."

"But you want to?"

"She's in trouble. Someone started the gas in her home, stayed inside, and planted listening devices. She needs help."

"What does Buck say?"

He sighed. "He said to lay off on both her and Randal's situations. With everything going on, I think he's worried about the team."

"He may be worried about the team, but there's more at stake here. I think you should go talk to her."

"She said to back off."

Danica scoffed. "She's scared. If she's got something else going on she doesn't want to talk about, then she's going to push you away. If you think she's in danger, then maybe you should go talk to her. Let her know you want to help."

"I don't even know where she went. She just left."

"Jeff, this isn't rocket science. You're over-analyzing it. Text her and ask if she's okay, see if she wants to meet for ice cream, or ask to pick her up."

"Ice cream? It's forty degrees outside."

Danica shrugged. "Trust me on this, ice cream always works when a woman is upset."

Before she could walk away, he took her hand and swung her backward. "So, were you going to tell me about this?" He pulled up her fingers and the large diamond on her left hand sparkled.

"Oh, that. Well, it just happened." She gave a grin. "We've not really told anyone, except Buck, of course."

"So that's where you were instead of training. Haiden asked Buck?"

Danica's cheeks flushed. "Yep. A few days ago."

He wrapped her in a hug. "I'm happy for you. Both of you. Wait, is that what was going on this morning?"

"I wasn't sure how to tell you. I was kinda hoping Haiden would say something."

"Did you think I wouldn't be excited for you? Really?" He shook his head. "I think it's great. Honestly. So, when's the big day?"

She chuckled and stepped back. "Actually, we're thinking of eloping."

"That fits." He gave her a wink. "Just let me know if you need help with interference. Buck might want to be the one to give you away."

"He's doing that already with Bex."

"Doing what?" Bexley walked through the doors with bags of groceries, Evan in tow.

Jeff grinned down at Danica as she turned bright red.

"What's going on?" Bex sat down the groceries, hands on her hips as she glared between them.

Knowing Dani's inability to be the center of attention, he pulled her hand up.

"Oh my goodness!" Bexley grabbed Dani in a hug. "I'm so excited for you!"

Evan chuckled from the island. "I need to have a talk with Haiden."

"Why?" Dani pulled away from Bex long enough to pin Evan with a glare.

"After the way I was attacked about Bexley last year? He deserves a ribbing."

"Oh yeah, that's right." Jeff winked at Evan as Bexley pulled Danica to the couch. "But I think it's great."

"I'm sure you do. Now, we've got to find someone for you."

He huffed and turned to Evan. "Don't start."

"Heard you were doing well with that doctor from the other day."

"Not so much now."

"Problems already?" Evan wore a grin as he leaned into the kitchen island. "I thought you were supposed to be the smart one around here?"

"Let me ask you something." Jeff leaned in, glancing over his shoulder at Bexley and Danica completely distracted in conversation. "How did you manage not knowing Bexley's past?"

"What?" Evan's face flushed as he straightened. "Why do you ask?"

"I know Shelby is holding back, and now, she's being harassed. Someone was in her home last night, left doors open and planted bugs."

"She was being spied on? Why?"

Jeff shrugged. "That's the thing, she says she doesn't know."

"But you think she does?"

Jeff nodded.

Evan let out a long breath. "You're going to have to either trust her on it or let her go."

"That's not what I was looking for."

"You can't force her to tell you, and if you go snooping, she'll know the second it does come up. It took forever for Bex to finally trust me with the things she'd been through. It doesn't happen all at once."

Jeff paced the kitchen.

"Jeff, if you think she's in trouble, go talk to her. Maybe she doesn't realize the stakes."

"Or she does and she doesn't want to tell me."

"Or that." Evan shrugged. "You barely know this woman. Is this because we helped her out and you feel responsible?"

"Not responsible. I asked her out before all of this happened. I figured out that day at the ER, she's impressive and smart and beautiful. I wanted to get to know her. I just don't understand why, after all the other stuff, she doesn't trust me."

"Then ask." Evan slapped him on the shoulder as he walked past and to the living room.

Pulling his phone from his back pocket, Jeff scrolled through to find Shelby's number.

Hey. I just wanted to check on you.

Tapping the countertop, bubbles flashed up and down and then disappeared on the screen.

I've heard ice cream heals all wounds. Would you like to join me?

Jaw clenching, he waited for the response to finally come through.

Yes.

Want me to pick you up or want to meet?

Where?

He frowned. So much for trying to be protective if he couldn't figure out where she was staying.

Coldstone on Montgomery.

I'm not sure where that is. It'll take me a bit.

I'll come get you. Remember, I'm very punctual.

Okay. I'm at the Marriott downtown.

On my way.

With a grin, he shoved the phone back into his pocket. "I'm out. Have Buck call if he needs me."

"Good luck!"

Sighing at Danica's comment, he headed out the door and slid into the SUV. "I'm going to need a lot more than luck," he mumbled.

17

Shelby nervously paced the hotel room, waiting for Jeff to let her know he was outside. "This is ridiculous."

Going out with Jeff was a bad idea. The detective was adamant about the danger she was causing, but there had to be an alternative to sitting around here watching T.V. Her mind would wander and then the fear and worry would drown every thought.

Besides, after all his years of training, surely he could keep them safe, right?

Letting out a sigh, she dumped the small pizza box into the trash can, her stomach turning at the remnants of the late lunch. She had forced herself to eat, but after everything that happened at the house, the detectives and their questions, it was just too much.

A knock sounded and she jumped. Calming her pounding heart, she tiptoed to the door and looked out the peephole. Jeff stood outside.

Unlatching the door, she pulled it partly open. "How did you know which room I was in?"

He shrugged with a grin. "I happen to know the guy that runs the front desk. I wanted to walk you down."

95

Chewing on the inside of her cheek, she couldn't make herself move.

"Shelby?"

"I ... I don't want to put you in any danger and the detective—"

"He's got issues with me and my team. You're not putting anyone in danger." He shook his head with a frown. "Do you want me to bring you something to eat instead of going out?"

"Why're you being so helpful?"

"What?"

"I mean, I've been nothing but trouble and you have to keep rescuing me all the time."

He chuckled and leaned a shoulder against the doorway. "Not trouble. I promise."

She blew out a deep breath. "Okay. Let me get my bag."

"It's windy, you might need a coat."

After grabbing her purse, she looked around and groaned.

"What?"

"I left my coat at home." Opening her duffle, she pulled out a windbreaker and slid it on.

"You're going to get cold in that. I think I have an extra coat in the car."

"This will be fine." Sliding the key card into her pocket, she followed him from the room.

"So, you still want ice cream? It's chilly out and we can always go for dinner."

"I'm not really all that hungry. Honestly, I just can't sit in that room anymore." She shoved the button for the elevator.

"A distraction? Well, you've come to the right guy."

She chuckled. "I'm glad you see it that way."

"I've got just the thing. It's not ice cream, but if you can make an exception, it'll be worth it."

Her eyebrow raised.

"No funny business. Just food. Promise."

Stifling a chuckle, she nodded. "Whatever you think is best."

After riding the elevator down in silence, Jeff's arm went around her waist as the doors opened and she tensed before she could stop herself.

"You okay?"

Licking her lips, she nodded as they stepped from the elevator. At the lobby doors, she paused, staring at the darkness around them. Thankfully, Jeff's arm went back around her waist and she sank in, arms crossed and shivering. Suddenly, all she could think about was him being there to protect her and keep her safe.

God, please watch over us.

"So, WHERE'RE WE GOING?" Shelby leaned against the middle console with a grimace.

"First, how's your back?"

"Just sore. It'll heal."

"Well, there's a great bakery I know about that I bet you've never been to. It's the best you've ever tasted."

"That sounds—"

"Amazing?" He glanced over with a grin. "Because it is."

"I was going to say ominous. It's like those commercials that promise the best food or music or the best entertainment and then you go and are completely disappointed."

"You live with a glass half empty, huh?"

She shot him a smirk. "I guess I just expect things to fail."

"Usually that's because you've had a few things fail in your life."

"Don't analyze me, Jeff Powers."

He let out a chuckle. "Sounds like you need a reality check."

She huffed and turned to him. "So, starting a new job in a new state and I've been through a knife fight and an abduction, now someone is bugging my home and I can't even stay at home because they tried to fill it with gas to explode. Does that sound like someone that needs a reality check?"

Hearing the quaver in her voice, he reached over and snatched up her hand. "Shelby, you've had something terrible happen and had a terrible few days. But it won't last forever. Morning is coming."

She sighed, her fingers squeezing his. "I know. Now I just feel like I'm whining."

"Not whining. You can vent to me. I can take it. Everyone needs someone they can talk to, get things out in the open. I'm available anytime you want to talk."

"Thanks," she whispered.

Her fingers trailed over his knuckles and his jaw clenched. Silence filled the car and at the light, he glanced over to see her focused on their hands.

"Shelby? What's going on? Why did you move here?"

"It was the only place I could get a job." Leaning her head back, she closed her eyes.

He forced his back to the road and headed downtown. *God, please help her open up, give me the words.*

Finally finding a parking spot downtown, he rushed her out of the truck.

"Jeff ... why the hurry?"

"I want to get there before they close. You cold?"

She shrugged. "A little."

"Then we can run. Come on."

Gripping her hand, he jogged down the sidewalk, pulling her behind them and smiling at her chuckle. After passing a few storefronts, he opened the door and led her inside.

"I didn't think about your back. Are you okay?"

She nodded, a smile on her face. "Yes. My back is fine."

"Good." He squeezed her hand and enjoyed the flush on her cheeks. "I wouldn't want to be too late."

"Jeffrey?"

"Yes, ma'am." He called as he pulled Shelby to the counter.

Nanna Rose came out from the back with a smile on her face. "There you are! You've been gone too long."

"I was here two days ago. But they said you were out that morning." He smiled as the woman leaned over the counter and grabbed his free hand.

"Yes, I was at the doctor's office. Now, who is your friend?"

"This is Shelby."

"Oh, how nice to meet you, Shelby."

Shelby offered her hand. "You too ... uh?"

"Nanna Rose, everyone calls me Nanna Rose." Rose winked and stepped to the glass case. "What do you want tonight?"

"One of each." He grinned as Nanna Rose laughed.

"You might have been able to do that once upon a time, but not now, I'm afraid."

His face heated as Shelby let out a chuckle. "She tends to have no filter." He smirked at the grin across Shelby's face.

"I don't need one. I'm old enough people should respect me."

"Yes, ma'am." He looked down at Shelby as they replied in unison.

"Now, enough chit-chat. I'm ready to close."

"I don't know if I can decide." Shelby smiled as she looked over the various pies and muffins that filled the glass case.

"It's all good. Trust me."

Getting their selections to go, he reluctantly drove her back to the hotel. It was too cold to sit outside, and he hadn't planned well enough to anticipate the bakery closing before they had time to sit down and eat.

Pulling into the parking lot, he opened her door and fought surprise as she slid down from the truck with both of their pie containers.

"You're not stealing that, right? Because I might have to fight you for it."

"Hmm. Normally I think I could take you. But my back is still sore."

He laughed out loud, following her inside the lobby and to the elevator.

"There's a sitting area in my room, if that's okay?"

"Better than outside or in the truck. Sorry we didn't make it in time to sit at the bakery."

"This is great, Jeff. Thanks for texting me."

He grinned as they stepped off the elevator and he took the containers from her so she could use her keycard.

"Let me just close my bag," she mumbled and zipped up her suitcase, then shut the bathroom door as he sat down on the couch. "I've got some water?"

"Perfect."

She sat down, handing him the water bottle as he handed her the coconut cream pie. After ripping open the plastic silverware, he watched as she took a bite.

"Oh, my, goodness." She looked up at him with wide eyes and he laughed.

"Told you it was good."

"Why has no one told me about this place? I mean, it's going to be detrimental to my health, but man, this is amazing."

"I started going there when I first joined the force. My first partner introduced me and I stop in at least once a week. But usually, I limit myself to just a coffee and the occasional muffin." He winked as she chuckled.

Watching her finish the piece of pie, he smiled. All the worry about being able to enjoy their time went out the window once they stepped on that elevator. She'd finally relaxed, eased up around him enough to look happy.

"You know, you do that a lot."

His eyes found hers. "Do what?"

"Stare."

Feeling his face heat, he nodded. "I'm sorry. I live inside my head sometimes, weighing my words."

She set her container on the coffee table and leaned back to watch him, chewing on the plastic fork. "And why do you live inside your head so much?"

"Remember I told you I learned early on to keep my mouth shut? That's what happens. I've got a lot going through my mind, and I need to really think it through before I say something I shouldn't."

"And what were you thinking through?"

He chuckled and set his container down. "Just a few questions."

"I don't believe that," she mumbled and took a sip of her water.

"Well, I do have questions. But if you want to vent or if you have questions, go ahead." He gave her a wink as he uncapped his water bottle.

"Why is the detective mad at you?"

That was a direct hit.

He cleared his throat. "It seems he's not a fan of our team."

"Why?"

With a sigh, he put down the water bottle. "About three months ago, one of our team was kidnapped by a cop."

"What?" She bolted upright with wide eyes. "I don't remember hearing about that. Who was it?"

"Danica."

She covered her mouth.

"It was an old family acquaintance. Long story short, he wanted revenge, and another friend had convinced him to help kidnap her."

"I can't imagine," she whispered. "But why would the detective be upset with you over that? It wasn't your fault or hers."

"It makes them look incompetent, a dirty cop that kidnaped a woman. There's also a lot of bad press from the last several months before that." Jeff shook his head. "Someone has been gunning for us, trying to make us look incompetent. He's just believing what he reads."

Shelby sat her water down. "So he's blaming you for that one situation? That doesn't seem right. It's not like all cops are bad. There's just this one that did something wrong."

Jeff shrugged. "So now, why don't you explain why he doesn't seem to like you very much."

Her cheeks flushed red. "It's a long story."

"I've got time." He leaned back against the couch to face her, her jaw clenching as she avoided eye contact. "Look, you don't have to tell me, Shelby. I'm not going to guilt you into it or anything. But I am worried. The doors being opened is one thing, the bugs … that's a whole new situation. Someone is trying very hard to get to you and I think you know why."

"But I don't," she shook her head as tears formed in her eyes. "I really don't. I've lived here for almost eighteen months, and I have some work friends and colleagues but no one that I've angered."

"No boyfriends?"

"Sure, every guy is thrilled to ask out a doctor that's constantly busy and has no time in her schedule." Wiping her cheeks, she took a deep breath. "Look, there's stuff that I had to get away from and I hope that's all you need. I don't want to get into it and I don't want to dwell on it. I just want this new life. My job is very important to me."

He took hold of her hand. "I can see that it is. I believe you, Shelby. If you ever want to discuss it, just let me know."

"Thanks," she mumbled.

He wiped a few tears from her cheek and tucked some stray hair behind her ear. "You didn't finish your pie."

"It's too much. I've got a fridge for later."

"Quitter."

"Trust me, it'll be gone by morning. It's not like I'm sleeping all that great. I'm sure I'll need a midnight snack."

He sighed and gave her hand a squeeze. "You want me to park outside? Or I can get a room across the hall."

Her eyes widened. "No, I mean ... I can't believe you would do that. You don't even know me."

"I know you well enough. What you've had to deal, it's terrible. You don't deserve to feel like this. If I can help, I want to."

Her mouth dropped. "I do appreciate that, but I'll survive."

"I know you will."

The tension increased as he sat there staring into her bright, amber eyes. If she hadn't been through so much ...

Her red lips parted and he took his cue. "I think I'll head out. See if you can get some sleep," he whispered.

She nodded and he stood, surprised she kept hold of his hand as she stood too. At the door, he paused as she opened it up.

Wrapping an arm around her shoulders, she came willingly, clinging to his sides as he gave her a hug.

"Call me if you need anything," he whispered, smiling at the shiver that shook her body once more.

"Thanks, Jeff."

A quick kiss on the top of the head and he stepped into the hallway. "If you lock it up, no one is getting in. Trust me. Breaking into a hotel room without a key and with the metal latches in place is a ton of work."

"Thanks for trying to make me feel better." She leaned against the doorframe with a grin.

"Anytime." He needed to leave, but the look on her face, her eyes darting about ...

Her head tilted to the side. "Jeff, tell me why you're so willing to risk so much. I mean, I appreciate it, but I have no idea why you would be so willing."

"You don't owe me anything." He stepped into her space. "I don't know if that's part of your past, but I'm not trying to get to you, Shelby. I'm not looking for payment, for a certain response. Just your friendship. I want you to be safe and I want to be friends." His eyes narrowed as she turned beet red once more.

"You deserve much more than someone just looking for something from you," he mumbled. "I understand you being careful, not just with who you're around but who you're putting your trust in. It's not like I haven't thought about who I'm putting my trust in."

Her eyes suddenly jutted to his. It was the truth. He was falling way too hard for a woman that was holding on to a lot. Hard enough he was starting to risk a little too much too soon.

"Be safe, Jeff," she whispered, her gaze bouncing from his lips to his eyes.

"You too."

Swallowing the urge to find out what she wanted from him, he turned and headed down the hallway to the elevator as fast as he could.

18

Wednesday Morning

"Sir, a package came for you."

Louis took the offered package and motioned for Patrice to leave. Once the door closed, he opened up the large envelope. A folder emerged with a post-it note attached:

I found this with Carver's things, thought you might want to take a look. You can call me back at his number.

Carefully opening the folder, Louis thumbed through pages of redacted information before landing on a familiar picture.

"Finally, an end in sight," he murmured.

The one thing that would bring down the TRT in a swift and efficient manner sat on his desk, ready to be unleashed.

Pulling out the phone, he dialed Carver's number.

"I take it you're pleased with the information?"

Louis huffed. "How'd you get this?"

"I've got a key to Carver's place and recently stopped by to see what I could find."

"The police searched it already after what happened."

"Not his other place. He's got an off-books apartment where he does his work. That stack of paperwork was sitting together with a lot of other pages. It all contained redacted material and I know he's not that tech-friendly. Seems he had some help hacking into a government facility."

Louis sat back in his chair. "And you are?"

"You can call me a friend."

"Looks like we have a deal."

"I'm currently tied up with another project, but a guy like me has to be ready when things like this drop into his lap."

"A project?"

"Yeah, it's personal."

Louis nodded. "Understood. What brings you to Dallas?"

"I've been in and out of this area for years. Made a few friends, one of them being Carver. I was on my way here when I heard the news."

"This information is important to me and I won't have a debt hanging over my head. You want to tell me what this information is worth?"

"I've heard through the grapevine you've made some new friends. Someone that is well cultured."

"Perhaps. Why do you ask?"

"I'd appreciate a good word."

"I don't know you."

"You will. I'll give you some information when it's time."

Louis huffed. "Just remember, I'm not a man to be crossed."

A cackle came from the line. "Man, I don't even know who I'm talking to. I'll be in touch."

The call ended and Louis put up the phone, staring down at the folder's contents. His end of the deal just became a reality.

———

STANDING at the bedside on the sixth floor, Shelby watched as the man from the ER started to wake.

"Mr. Quarters?"

His eyes fluttered some more before they finally opened, his eyebrows knitted together.

"What happened?"

"You were attacked in the ER. Do you remember coming in?"

The dark-haired man groggily searched the room, then groaned as he tried to sit up.

"Sir, you need to sit back."

His eyes widened as they focused on her. "You."

"Do you remember me?" Shelby waited as the man took several large breaths, then leaned back. "Sir?"

"Can I have some water?"

"I'll have the nurse bring you some ice, okay?"

The man nodded, his gaze dropping from hers.

"Do you remember what happened?"

Shaking his head, Terry glanced at her and then at the wall. "I ... I'm not sure."

"Do you know why you came to the emergency room?"

"No."

His clipped answer made her frown. Besides the wound in his arm and a bump on the head from Randal, she had found no other problems. All the tests, the possible brain or heart problems, everything was negative.

"Ice?"

"Of course." She headed out of the room and to the nurses' station. "Talia? Can you get Mr. Quarters some ice?"

"He finally woke?"

"Yeah, he's still confused."

"Did he remember anything?"

Shaking her head, Shelby sat down at the table. "I mean, I don't understand why he came into the ER in the first place. None of the tests came back positive for anything. He has some high cholesterol and his BP is off, but nothing that would warrant a trip to the ER."

"Maybe he was having chest pains or something."

"The woman that admitted him said he just needed to see me and the only thing he'd say is that he was hurting. If it was that severe, she would've sent him back."

"Don't worry, Shelby. I'm sure it was just one of those coincidences. I'll get him taken care of."

"Thanks."

Coincidence or not, the man was a mystery. Maybe the police would have better luck getting through to him. Dialing the detective's number on the hospital phone, she leaned against the table.

"Fredricks."

"Hi, this is Dr. Durning. Mr. Quarters is awake."

"How awake? Can I talk to him?"

"Of course." She rolled her eyes. "I wouldn't have called if he wasn't completely competent. But he said he doesn't remember me or anything that happened."

"Let us do our jobs, Dr. Durning. Thank you for doing yours. We'll be there soon. When will he be released?"

"With what he's been through, he's very weak and will need to take his time even getting out of bed. I'd say at least another week. But it's up to the lead physician. I just happened to be here."

"We'll be there shortly."

The call ended and she hung up the receiver. Maybe he was right. The police detective would be better at questioning the man. But Mr. Quarters did appear to be lying when he said he didn't know why he came to the ER that day.

A chart was thrust into her vision and she let out a sigh and stood.

Give me strength, God. I just need a little more patience to finally be where I need to be.

STEPPING from the parking lot of the coffee shop, Jeff paused at the dark sedan facing the building.

"Jeff?"

He glanced up at Evan and the sedan sped away.

"Who was that?"

"I don't know," he mumbled as Evan stared at the black car. "For some reason, I keep seeing one like it. I'm not sure if it's just me or a coincidence."

"How many times?"

Jeff turned to Haiden. "Twice. Yesterday and today."

"Coincidence. Do you know if it's the exact same?"

Jeff shrugged and headed toward the SUV. "Nope. Didn't get a good look yesterday."

"Was this yesterday when you were helping a certain doctor?" Evan let out a chuckle. "I'm betting you were distracted."

"It was at her house after we found the bugs."

Evan winced. "Did the detective call and let you in on that?"

"No. I don't think he'll tell me. He's apparently upset with the TRT after what happened with Dani."

Haiden let out a scoff.

"Even if he does find out, chances of actually getting a trace on whoever put them there is slim. I did hear the tech say there were no fingerprints in her apartment where the bugs were found or on the doorknobs, light fixtures, security pad." Jeff shook his head as he pulled onto the highway. "It's like whoever did it wanted her to know they were there but didn't leave a trace."

"You think they wanted her to know about it? To what end?" Evan questioned.

"To distract her."

Jeff glanced at Haiden in the back seat. "Distract?"

Haiden shrugged. "Or upset her. It's a game."

"That's what I'm thinking." Jeff's jaw tightened. "Someone is setting her up for a fall or trying to ruin her career. Whatever she's left in her past is bad enough she's run away from it. I'm just wondering if it's found her."

"So she's running?"

Jeff glanced at Evan. "She mentioned trying to get away from some things."

"You better watch your back." Evan rumbled. "That black sedan is a sign. You see it again, you need to be careful."

"I think they're after her, not me. Besides, like Haiden said, it's more than likely a coincidence."

"It's not a coincidence that we go for coffee and a Bible study every Wednesday morning, to this shop at this time," Haiden commented from the back seat.

Jeff nodded. "You're right. We need to be more observant."

"You mean *you* need to be more observant. Haiden and I know all about each car parked in front of the diner and how many people were in the café."

"Six women, thirteen men, three waitresses, and at least two cooks in the back. There was a delivery van that came in twenty minutes after we sat down."

"Good grief. How long you plan on doing that?"

"Being observant?" Evan chuckled. "Ask Buck."

As the men discussed how blatantly unobservant he was, Jeff couldn't help but wonder if they had a point. If someone was coming after Shelby and saw them being friendly, maybe they were coming after him too.

And as much as she was holding back about her past, she wasn't holding back about what was happening to her now. He believed her completely that she had no idea who was bugging her house and keeping her doors open.

Glancing at the mirrors, his alert went up. If that black car was following them, watching, he needed to be on guard. And that meant Shelby needed to be on guard as well.

19

Standing inside the door to the patient's room, Shelby did her best to stay out of Terry Quarter's vision but close enough to hear what was being said.

"Do you recognize this man?" Detective Fredricks questioned.

"Um, looks familiar. I just can't place the name."

"Randal Goodwin."

Terry nodded. "Okay, yeah. That sounds right. What about him?"

"Why did you attack him?"

"What? I didn't attack anyone. I'm the one in bed."

"Mr. Quarters, I've seen the video. You intercepted Mr. Goodwin, sat down right next to him."

"I might've recognized him from somewhere, but I didn't start nothin'." Terry let out a huff. "I'm tired."

"Just a few more questions. Recognize him?"

Shelby glanced around the curtain to see Terry's eyebrows furrowed, holding the picture and studying it. "No, I don't think I do. Who is he?"

"You don't recognize him at all?"

Terry shook his head.

"What about the name Dierks Carver?"

"Nope."

Fredricks leaned a hip against the edge of the hospital bed. "Mr. Quarters, I'd like to advise you that telling the truth right now will save you down the road."

"I can't tell you what I don't know."

Fredricks took the pictures. "We'll let you rest a bit. But I'll be back later."

"Maybe I should call a lawyer. It's like you don't believe me."

"I don't."

With that, Detective Fredricks and Detective Alton pushed past her out the door. She followed.

"That's it?"

Detective Fredricks turned with a frown. "What?"

"A man tried to kill me to get to him and you're going to stand there and say 'what'? I want to know why he asked for me and why all this happened." Crossing her arms, she held in the sickness swirling through her stomach.

"Dr. Durning, we'll get to the bottom of things. It does take time, especially when he's in the hospital room and not at the police station. I'll give him some time to think on it and then we'll discuss it with him again." He turned to the other detective. "Get his phone lines tapped. I want to know if he makes any calls."

"What about me?"

"I suggest you act as if nothing's happened. If he does remember why he asked for you, maybe he'll share that information once he's more comfortable."

"Comfortable? The man is obviously lying, even I can see that. He lied to me before you guys got here and now you want to wait him out? What if someone else shows up and another person is put in danger?"

Fredricks motioned down the hallway. "I'll get a guard posted on the floor just in case. As for now, you can keep your distance and let me know if he does mention anything pertinent."

She nodded as the detectives left. Her job was to save lives, protect those she could. Taking a deep breath, she closed her eyes and leaned against the wall a moment. Save lives, protect those who needed help. It was her purpose in this life. She knew that as well as she knew the sky was blue.

Then why was God putting so many roadblocks to keep her from doing it?

AFTER THREE MEETINGS with investors and another interview, Louis was finishing up the rest of the day's work when a buzzing came from his desk drawer.

"What?"

"I've heard some things."

"Like?"

"Dierks had a bad way of letting things go. He'd sometimes let people slip away, un-noticed."

"Hmmf. What do I know about it?"

"Come now. I thought we were becoming business partners."

At the comment, Louis's jaw clenched.

"Look, I've got ears around town and I've heard of a few loose ends. One just woke up in the hospital."

"And how is that my problem?"

"He knows Dierks. And if he knows Dierks, he knows all the same things I know about Dierks. His friends, his connections, his involvement."

"Are you saying this could become a situation?"

"Could be. But I'd be willing to handle it for you."

Louis leaned back, puffing on his cigar for a moment. "There is one man, he eludes us all. The police can't find him, my people can't find him. He knows too much."

"I'll make a deal. Payment for one job, but I'll do two."

"Payment?"

"Same deal you had with Dierks. But I'll actually do my job."

"Seems convenient for you to want to help so easily. Why is that?"

"Do you remember me mentioning meeting your friends?"

Louis frowned. "Yes."

"It's time. I have a score for them as payment from a previous situation. One that went wrong in too many ways. I won't be welcomed back without payment in full. I can offer that and more. But I need someone to convince your friend to keep his cool."

A chuckle escaped his lips. "You screwed up so bad you have to ask me to stop them from killing you? And I'm supposed to trust you?"

"I provided, didn't I? I gave you everything you wanted."

"Then why don't I just walk away now? Forget you even exist. You showed your hand too early."

"Check your phone."

Louis's phone vibrated. "You idiot. This line can be traced."

On the screen sat the words:

I KNOW WHO YOU ARE, MAYORAL CANDIDATE ROLTZ.
PERHAPS YOU'D LIKE FOR ME TO SHARE.

The air thinned as all the messages between him and Dierks Carver filled the screen. Everything that linked the TRT to him, all the things he was trying to do to get rid of them, sat there in black and white.

"I'm not a hired idiot, Roltz. All I ask for is protection. You do that for me, I'll make all this go away."

Swallowing the bile as his heart pounded, Louis shoved his cigar into the ashtray. "Fine. But if you mess this up, step out of line even once, I will bury you myself."

After hitting the red button, he slammed the phone on the desk and stood. Even in death, Dierks Carver would be a thorn in his side. This had to end.

Snatching up the phone once more, he placed a call.

"You have news?"

"I have answers. But I do have someone you want."

"I doubt that," the accent-laced rumble etched out. "Who?"

"Someone that wants me to vouch for him. He apparently made a mess of things for you a few years ago and now wants to make amends."

"Too many to count. What kind of amends?"

"I'll send you his number and you can discuss that."

Silence stretched.

"This man, he has something on you?"

Louis frowned. "Yes."

"If I meet with him, you care what happens to him?"

"No."

The call ended and Luis forwarded the number. If this 'friend' of Dierks wanted so badly onto the playing field, he would have to prove himself. And his new Russian friend was the man to make that decision.

Less work for him, more protection. All he needed now was the TRT out of the way and the race was his.

20

"So, tell me about last night."

Jeff couldn't hide his grin as he sat in the diner with Buck. After a long morning of drills, they had left the couples to their own business and stopped for lunch.

"First, where's Sergio?"

"Asked for some time. He said he's got some family issues, needs to be there for them." Buck sat down his mug. "So, spill."

"Well, it wasn't what I was hoping for, but it's a start."

Buck frowned.

"Look, Shelby's been through a lot and she's frustrated. Seems there's some things going on in her past, things she doesn't want to discuss."

"That's a red flag."

"No, it's a past. I've got one too, remember?" Jeff took a few sips of the water in front of him. "I'm not ready to share and I don't expect her to either."

"Is it related to the doors and the gas leak?"

"I doubt it. When I brought it up again, she was more than distraught about what happened. I do believe that if she knew who it was, she'd tell Fredricks."

"Mind if I sit?"

The chair pulled out and Captain Marty DeSalis sat down.

"Sure." Buck's eyes narrowed at the sudden arrival of the police captain. "What's got you out and about, Marty?"

"Coffee?"

Marty nodded to the waitress and waited until she left to take a sip. "How's your girl?"

"Dani's doing well." Jeff's jaw clenched until it ached.

The memory filled his mind, making his heart pound and bile fill his throat. Danica kidnapped by Burnett, then disappeared as they found Burnett dead. Marty had taken over the case, kept them involved as much as possible.

Marty leaned into the table, pushing his mug to the side. "I know you're on thin ice with the commish right now, but I have some info you need to know."

"Thin ice?" Jeff frowned at Buck.

"He's not happy with me currently."

"What'd you do?"

Buck glared a moment at Jeff before looking over at Marty. "What info?"

"There's been a big push lately, we've had a lot of arrests in east Dallas. Drugs."

Buck shrugged. "What's that got to do with us?"

"The commish sent out a report today. There's a new dealer pushing his way into the area. They're anticipating a lot of retaliation, a lot of problems on the street."

"Again, what's it got to do with us? We're not cops." Jeff crossed his arms.

"We've had a few run-ins regarding these guys. The crew is filled with Russian-speaking men, ruthless." Marty took a sip of coffee. "But what I wanted to speak to you about is the fact we can't keep these men in jail."

Jeff leaned into the table. "What do you mean?"

"We get the evidence, the DA gets involved, and before we

can get them in front of a judge, they're out the door. The DA says we've had too many technicalities, a piece of paper that wasn't signed off, evidence that goes missing. There's something going on and I don't know who to talk to."

"We're already on every cop's radar after what happened with Burnett. We're not the guys to help."

Marty shook his head at Jeff. "The same situation that you dealt with a few months ago seems to be rubbing off on us now."

"You'll have to be more specific. Situations from a few months ago were many." Buck gritted.

"The media is labeling us incompetent, unable to get the bad guys off the streets. Every day I'm dealing with another reporter asking the same questions and we're taking hits."

"And the commish?" Jeff questioned.

Marty narrowed his eyes. "What about him?"

"Have you spoken to him about what's going on?"

Marty took a long sip of his coffee and cut his eyes to the window.

"You think he's involved?" Buck mumbled.

"All I know is that one day, everything was fine; the next, we've lost three major drug players to a technicality."

Buck leaned back in his chair. "The mayor's not going to get involved in any way while the election is right around the corner. He's on the election trail until after November. But the commissioner, I did wonder why when we were going through so much difficulty, he wasn't backing us up."

Marty chuckled. "What in the world did you do to get on his bad side, Buck?"

"He's suddenly too busy to talk to me, to take an interest in something he helped me create. He was a good friend, and I expected a good friend to reach out after Dani went missing."

"So, what now?" Marty asked.

Jeff huffed. "I guess you better start cinching up these technicalities. Then there won't be any excuses."

Marty shook his head. "If they're getting away with this much, what happens when we start losing undercover officers, informants, men and women that get taken out because someone is giving up information? I don't want to figure it out after I lose my people. Someone is talking and I don't know who to trust."

Buck worked his jaw back and forth, then nodded to Jeff. "Keep your eyes open, Marty. And when you get something on Dale Fletcher, you let me know." Buck stood. "If I find something out, you'll be the first call I make."

"Thanks."

Stepping outside, Jeff scanned the area, focusing on the same black car Buck was staring at with a fisted hand.

"Tell me that's a friend of yours."

"Not mine."

The dark sedan had tinted windows and a distorted front plate, uncomfortably familiar. "I've seen it before."

Buck turned to him. "Where?"

"Last night and then early this morning, after we left the coffee shop. You think it could possibly be Dale Fletcher?" Jeff questioned as he continued his search of the area. "Maybe trying to finish what he started?"

"Not him. My guys are on him. He's in Nevada now."

"What?" Jeff turned to Buck. "And when were you going to tell me?"

"Not your problem."

"The one man left after everything went down with Danica, all the attacks on our office, and it's not my problem?"

The car started and sped away, running through the red light and narrowly avoiding a mini-van.

"You know who that was?"

Buck shook his head as Marty walked up behind them.

"The tags were blacked out."

"We noticed," Jeff called over his shoulder as they headed for Buck's truck.

"Was it the same as this morning?"

Jeff shrugged. "Not sure, didn't get a good look and I wasn't paying attention."

"Start paying attention."

Jeff gritted his teeth at Buck's comment and slid into the truck.

Riding along back to the office, Jeff mulled over the past three months. Adil Garrison, Thomas Eller, and Dale Fletcher. Three names he couldn't get out of his mind. When Danica was kidnapped, it connected to her past and Oscar Burnett, a dirty cop, and an old friend, Tony Carlyle.

Tony was in jail and Oscar was dead. But the other three names were behind the attacks that almost ruined the Tactical Response Team.

Thomas Eller was the caller of a phony kidnapping, the scene of Danica's genuine one. Adil Garrison, the man caught on camera outside the TRT setting up the bombs that were all boom and no destruction. They both ended up dead and all the attacks on the TRT ended. But what about Dale Fletcher?

"You know, I think Frazier owes us an explanation for all his silence."

"The police commissioner? You think you should go bother him if he's already upset with you?"

"He's not arrested me yet."

"Great. Let's just show up unannounced and make a scene. That'll go well with the police and the media."

"Sometimes, Jeff, you've got to push the boundaries."

"I like the boundaries. That's why I became an officer of the law."

Buck chuckled. "We'll try it your way first. Make the call."

With a sigh, Jeff pulled out his phone and searched for the commissioner's office number. If they could get an appointment, it would be in their favor. But if they couldn't get in, well, he knew how well that would play out.

"Dallas County Commissioner's Office. How may I direct

your call?"

"Commissioner Stonewall's office, please."

"Hold."

This was a bad idea.

21

S helby smiled at the text on her screen.

Hope to see you tonight. If you're not too busy and tired after work.

Jeff's text was a wonderful reprieve from the fear attacking her heart and mind lately. It seemed God's timing was finally proving itself.

"What's that smile for?" Talia grinned as Shelby slid the phone into her pocket.

"Nothing. Just a text from a friend."

"Just a friend?" Talia shook her head. "You know, I saw you talking to a tall, blonde-haired hunk on Sunday. He seemed quite taken with you."

"And how do you know that?"

"If a guy smiles at you the way he did, he's smitten. I'd take advantage."

Shelby couldn't help her grin.

"Is he the guy?"

"Actually, yes. He's been very helpful lately."

Talia's eyebrow perked. "Was he here when ..."

Shelby nodded as Talia trailed off.

"So a real hero too. You better make sure he knows you're interested."

"And how do you know I'm interested?"

Talia chuckled. "You need a book on body language. You smiling at your phone like that and him smiling at you, get with it!"

Shelby laughed as Talia spun and headed down the hallway. Pulling out her phone, she texted back.

> Of course. I'll let you know when I'm headed out.

Then I'll come walk you to your car.

She smiled at his concern.

> You don't have to do that. It might be late.

Not a problem. See you tonight.

> *Thanks, Jeff.*

Her heart pounded as she put the phone away. It had been years since she trusted herself around any man. It was a lustful, selfish relationship with Ryan, and it proved her completely oblivious. There was no way she would put herself through that again.

But with Jeff, it was different. He was a different man with morals and ideals. She had thought the same of Ryan.

God, what am I doing?

Trusting a man with her heart. A man that had saved her life, had shown up at a moment's notice just to protect her; he was proving himself worthy.

So why was her stomach churning and a lump forming in her throat at the thought of something more with him?

PACING THE OFFICE, Jeff glanced at the framed pictures and plaques that lined the wall. "How long have you known him?" He turned to Buck who was standing in the middle of the room, arms crossed.

"Years. He was a good friend after boot camp and the first couple of years in the Army. He always had a great head on his shoulders but decided the Army wasn't his home. Up until now, I'd disagreed with that decision."

Jeff chuckled as the door opened.

"I'm pretty busy, Buck. Wish you'd made an appointment."

Buck turned as Frazer only greeted him with a nod, then strode behind the large desk to sit down. His eyes leveled on Jeff and he frowned.

"Tried. You apparently don't have time."

"So you thought you'd just push your way into my schedule, huh?" Frazier leaned back in his oversized chair, his gaze shifting to Buck. "What do you need?"

"I don't need anything. I wanted to ask how things were going." Buck sat down on the edge of the chair as Jeff stood behind him. "You're jumpy. What's up?"

Frazer scoffed. "I'm not jumpy. I'm busy. Big difference."

"I left over a dozen messages for you a few months ago and you've yet to ask about Dani. You've always asked how she was doing."

"Heard she was found and things were good. I was told there was something going on with her and one of your guys. That's gonna cause trouble."

"The only trouble that comes around is when I found out who hired those men to mess with my team."

"Hang on. I thought that was Burnett and the other guy, Tony something."

Buck shook his head. "You know what I'm talking about. I can read it all over your face."

"What?"

"Buck," Jeff mumbled, taking a few steps as Buck leaned onto the desk.

"Tell me you had no idea."

Frazer's jaw jumped. "Idea about what?"

"Whatever those men were up to put us on alert to an attack on the TRT. Danica was left standing taken because our focus was elsewhere. If you have something to say, now would be the time."

Frazer stood. "I think you should go. You're messing with things you need to keep your nose out of. And don't think I don't know about your little fishing scheme. I'm not happy about that and you're lucky I don't charge you."

"Why don't you?"

"I'm giving you the benefit of the doubt," Frazer gritted out. "But that curtesy won't last past today. I can assure you."

"Let's go."

His face and neck bright red, Buck tromped out the door.

Jeff caught the keys Buck tossed and slid in behind the wheel. Allowing his mentor to calm, he let the silence stretch as they drove back to the office.

"What was he talking about?"

"What?"

Jeff frowned. "What kind of fishing scheme? Why would he put you in jail?"

"It's a long story. But I am wondering why I'm still standing if he knows about it. I thought I covered my tracks."

Jeff let out a groan as he leaned back in the seat. "You go to jail and we're done. You get that, right?"

"When Dani went missing and Frazier didn't even offer to help. I knew he had something else going on. At the time, I was determined to find out if it had anything to do with her disappearance."

"Did it?"

"Never saw a thing about it. But I didn't have time to go through it all. There were a lot of files."

Files? Buck had stolen files? Great, just great.

22

Shelby grinned as Jeff appeared from the hallway and leaned against the desk at the nurse's station.

"You ready?"

"Yes, give me a second to clock out." She turned and headed for the back hallway, sliding her name badge through the timeclock.

"You shouldn't let him walk around un-accompanied," Talia mumbled as she walked by, coat in her arm.

"I'll remember that for next time." Shelby winked and headed back to the front to see a few nurses grilling him. "I'm ready."

"Let's go." He took hold of her hand and eased her to the elevators.

She let out a chuckle as they stood at the elevator. "In a hurry?"

"Just, uh, avoiding more questions." He grinned down at her.

"Questions? Like?"

"Just kinda personal stuff."

Stifling a chuckle, she leaned against the back of the elevator. "I promise, next time if you want to walk me out, I'll meet you at the door instead."

He turned and leaned in close. "I don't mind questions. I'd just rather give answers to you than them."

Clenching her jaw at the need to shiver, she took a deep breath. "Noted."

His arm wrapped around her waist as they walked out and she settled in, completely trusting Jeff to protect her.

"Rough day?"

"No, just long. I'm fine."

"You don't act like it."

"I'm sorry. Things feel upside down and I'm trying to ..."

"Trying to what?" He held out his hand and she dug through her purse, finding the keyfob and placing it in his palm.

Jeff started the car as they finished crossing the lot. He unlocked the door and opened it for her, allowing her to slide inside.

"You didn't finish that thought." He stood in the space with a smirk, looking so good.

"This might be one of those thinking-it-through moments."

"Then how about you fill me in once we get to your hotel."

"I'll consider it."

He chuckled and handed her the keyfob, then closed the door.

Barely able to focus on the road, her mind swam with all that could go wrong so quickly if she told Jeff everything. It wasn't just a bad relationship, it was a terrible life. Those few years spent with Ryan were full of mistakes and decisions she couldn't take back.

Pulling into the hotel, she slid from the car as Jeff stood staring at the parking lot.

"Something wrong?"

It took a moment for his gaze to find hers as a black sports car sped through, tires squealing as it turned from the lot.

"It's fine," he mumbled, taking hold of her hand. "Let's get inside."

As they walked through the lobby and to the elevator, she pushed the third-floor button.

"You don't happen to know who drives a black mustang with tinted windows, do you?"

"You mean that car that drove out of here?"

He nodded.

"I don't think I've noticed one car that any of my friends drive."

He chuckled and pulled her hand in his as the doors opened. Once more guiding her down the hall, she leaned in, more than grateful that he was there.

At her door, she paused, pulling the keycard from her purse.

"You have some thoughts to share?"

"What were the questions they were asking you?"

He shrugged, then leaned a shoulder against the wall. "Just basic, how long have you lived here, what do you do, things like that."

She slowly nodded.

"But you already know most of that."

"So, what questions were you wanting me to ask?"

"Whatever you want to ask."

"That seems unlikely," she chuckled and unlocked her door. "I mean, you can't possibly mean any question." Tossing her purse on the coffee table she turned as Jeff straightened, an envelope in his hand. "What's that?"

"I don't know. It was under your door. Were you expecting some paperwork?"

Shaking her head, she took the envelope and pried open the tab. Pictures filled the inside, and one by one, she pulled them out.

Jeff took one. "Shelby."

She stared at the picture in his hand. There she stood in her kitchen, cooking.

"No," she whispered, her gut churning.

"I'm calling Fredricks."

Pouring out the rest of the pictures, her heart raced at the shots of her walking through the living room and kitchen in a towel, in just her workout clothes, then her pajamas.

"He's on his way," Jeff mumbled from behind her and she turned over several of the pictures. "Shelby?"

Sprinting to the bathroom, she heaved the contents of her stomach and then collapsed on the floor.

Who would do this? What had she done to make someone so vindictive and how far would they go?

JEFF PACED THE SITTING AREA, doing his best to keep from busting down the door to the bathroom. But Shelby was adamant he stay put.

She walked out, the smell of mint trailing along behind.

"Sorry, I just—"

"Don't apologize." He pulled her into a hug, her body leaned fully into his.

"Mr. Powers." Detective Fredricks walked in, a frown on his face. "I've spoken to the front desk, and they've already got the video pulled up. I'm assuming you know something about that?"

"I know the guy that runs this hotel, yeah. I asked if he could get it ready for you. The envelope is over there, I touched it and so did she."

Fredricks nodded and went to the bed, pulling on a pair of gloves. "Just the living room and kitchen?"

"Yes, that's all I saw," she mumbled.

Jeff gave her a squeeze. "You need to find a new place. You can stay at our office if you want. We can offer protection."

"No." She stepped back and wiped her face. "I mean, thanks, but I don't want to drag you into this too."

"You're not."

"I agree. Fewer people involved, the better." Fredricks straightened, envelope in hand. "I'll post an officer outside your house tonight. I'm sure it will be safe to go back with the police presence from yesterday as well as an officer outside." He walked away, phone to his ear.

"Shelby, I think you need more than just one officer in a car outside your house."

She sighed and sat on the edge of the bed. "I ... I have no idea what's going on." Her red-rimmed eyes looked up at him. "I can honestly say there's no one I know that would do this. How did they know where I was?"

"You're being followed." The black mustang peeling out of the parking lot earlier piqued his interest. "Have you noticed anyone watching you? Making you feel uncomfortable?"

"No. I mean, I'm usually pretty vigilant about that kind of thing. But to be honest, between the hospital and the clinic, I can't even tell you how many patients I've seen. Not that I wasn't paying attention to them, but there could've been someone else there while I worked and I don't think I would notice."

"This is important, Shelby." He attempted to ease the irritation building. "I'm asking you to come to my office, stay there with Danica and the rest of my team. Things are escalating—"

"Jeff." She stood with a huff. "The detective is adamant about keeping me safe, and I think you being around would make it worse for you and the team. I don't want to put you or anyone else in danger. I can't do that. It's not your job."

"It is too."

She offered a forced chuckle, shoving her hair behind her ears. "No, your job is to help people in bad situations, keep people safe during scary times."

"This is scary." He took hold of her hand.

"Yes, but it's my situation, not yours." She licked her lips and leaned forward. "Jeff, if anyone finds out I'm in protective custody, it'll ruin my reputation. I could lose my job at the hospital and the clinic if they think I've got something going on. I can't risk it."

"Your life is more important than a job."

She shook her head. "It's not easy to bounce back after something like this. Trust me, I can't just pick up the pieces and find another job. It took me so long last time." She pushed past him.

Watching her gather her things, he couldn't understand why she was so willing to act like nothing was wrong. And what happened last time? Was this the second time she'd had a stalker, and that's why she wasn't interested in getting help again? Could the person responsible have followed her here?

As she finished her bag, he took it from her hands.

"You said you've already been through this?"

Her wide eyes met his. "No, I mean, I've moved before. But I've never had a stalker or whatever this is."

"I need you both downstairs to look over the footage."

Jeff nodded to Fredricks from the doorway. Taking hold of Shelby's waist, he escorted her to the downstairs lobby.

"Hey, man. Everyone okay?"

Jeff shook Kirk's outstretched hand. "Yeah, we're okay. Thanks for getting this all together so quick."

"No problem. Usually, we watch out for people we don't recognize coming in, but there's a lot of people in and out right now."

He nodded to Kirk and they gathered around the computer.

"Here's the footage. Keep your eye on the guy in the hoodie."

The video played, showing several people exiting the elevator, including a man carrying a large envelope and wearing a hoodie.

"He came from the elevators and even here," Kirk switched the camera angle. "He's got his head down."

"You recognize him?"

"You're kidding, right?" Shelby shook her head. "I can't even tell what color hair he has or if he's even a he."

"No gait issues, no looking over his shoulder. He knew she

wouldn't be there," Jeff mumbled as he leaned in. "It's a man, looks like he has a beard or goatee."

The figure took a moment to shove the envelope under the door, then took off down the hallway and out the stairwell.

"We're checking the door for prints, but seeing how this is a hotel, we're not hopeful."

Shelby let out a deep sigh at Fredrick's comment.

"And no one with a hoodie like that entered from the front?" Jeff turned to Kirk.

"I've not gone over all of it. It could be earlier than in the last few hours."

"Send it to me, I'll go through and see if he's on any of the other cameras. He can't just be on the floor camera and that's all. He's not a ghost."

It made no sense. Why risk being seen just to prove to Shelby she'd been watched? The pictures could've been sent to her home and delivered by the post office. Why risk so much?

His mind rushed through training, his schooling, the other cases he had worked—there had to be a connection between Shelby and that man on the screen.

"There's something else there," he mumbled, memories of the past few days adding up in his mind, clicking into place. He didn't know the man's name, but he did know what he was driving. And he'd seen that car more than once.

23

"Kirk, do you have cameras at the parking lot?" Jeff questioned.

"Sure, why?"

"Just a hunch."

"Mind sharing?" Fredricks commented.

"There's a black Mustang I've seen a few times. It just seems ... odd. It was here when we showed up and then took off out of the lot."

"Yeah, I remember seeing him pull in."

"Him?" Jeff turned to Kirk.

Kirk nodded. "A guy stepped out and came inside with a duffle bag, but the wasn't dressed the same as the guy in the video."

Jeff frowned as the video played and the Mustang pulled in. "What's the time stamp?"

"Uh, 6:40."

"What time does the man shove the envelope under the door?" Fredricks questioned.

Kirk switched screens. "Almost seven."

"Play the video. If I'm right, it's our guy. He used the duffle for the hoodie and envelope, probably stashed it somewhere."

A man finally pulled himself from the car, bending into the back seat before he straightened.

"Recognize him?"

"No, I have no idea."

A large man with red hair, a goatee, and a black bag. He casually took his time putting the bag over his shoulder, running his hand through his rusty hair before slamming the car door and heading toward the hotel lobby.

"Here he is entering the hotel." Kirk clicked a button and the frame froze, a clear picture of the man.

"Send me that. I can run facial recognition, and maybe we can get a name."

"Got it."

Jeff let out a breath. "Fast forward to when he leaves. We pulled in about seven forty."

Kirk nodded.

Shelby leaned into Jeff, her body shaking. Wrapping an arm around her waist, she turned with a heavy sigh.

"Here it is, seven forty."

The video stopped and the hooded man appeared from the right-hand side of the screen, sliding into the car.

"It's him, it's all connected." Jeff looked to Fredricks. "That same Mustang was parked at Shelby's house when we found the bugs. It was from a distance, but he pulled out and followed her down the road. This morning, it was outside a café where Buck and I ate. It blew through a red light. We thought it was someone else."

"Someone else?"

"Another case," Jeff mumbled, hoping to keep from going into detail.

"Give me the address. I can get the video of the light and we can get confirmation."

"The tags are blacked out," Kirk commented.

"Yeah, same at the café. I'm not sure it will matter, it's probably stolen."

"With a clear shot of his face, we should be able to get a name if he's in the system. In the meantime, I'll get a list together, see who in Ms. Durning's circle drives a black Mustang."

"But I don't recognize him at all."

Fredricks shrugged as he texted on his phone. "It could be a friend of the guy that was doing him a favor in case you showed up."

"You really think it's someone I know? Like, personally?"

"Statistically, it's a friend, colleague, someone you've never thought twice about being around. They've taken an interest and you never even knew it."

Shelby paled and covered her mouth. "I just can't ... I can't imagine anyone being like that."

"I'll get a tech crew together to sweep the hotel for the bag and hat, see what we can come up with. You can take her home. I've had my guys clear the house and they'll be parked right outside for now."

"And later?" Jeff questioned as Fredricks shrugged.

"Guess we'll have to see what we can come up with."

Shaking his head, Jeff slapped Kirk on the shoulder. "Thanks for the help."

"Anytime. Tell Buck I said hi."

Jeff nodded and led Shelby from the hotel and to her car. "You want me to drive you and then we can come get it later?"

"I'm fine to drive," she mumbled, staring at the car, her hands clenching her purse.

"Hold this." He handed off her duffle bag and did a quick search under the car and around it. "Keys?"

She tossed the keyfob to him and he opened the car, turning it on.

"You're good to go. I'll follow."

"Jeff."

"No, I'm following you. Get in." He shut her door and waited until she started forward out of the lot before going to his car.

"Thanks for the answers, God."

Getting the guy's face, possibly his prints from the pictures or envelope, they could have the stalker within a few hours and this entire thing would be over. Judging by the strain on her face, she was trying way too hard to pretend it was all nothing.

Pulling behind her in the drive, she left the garage door open and he walked inside. He took the duffle bag from the back seat and closed the garage door. The police met him in the living room.

"We cleared it per Fredrick's orders. But he said something about a camera?"

Jeff nodded. "I only saw one picture, it looked like it was angled from here." He pointed to the corner of the room.

"Um, yeah, looks about right. You can see the living room and kitchen."

Scanning the corner, he slid his hand behind the curtain rod, feeling a hole. Taking down the curtain rod, he frowned at the two holes in the sheetrock.

"Looks like he took it down when he planted the bugs. It's not here." Setting down the rod, he motioned toward the door to the officers.

"We'll be right outside if you need anything, ma'am."

"Thanks." She straightened, offering a smile as the officers waved.

As they left, Jeff wrapped her in a hug. "Let me stay on your couch."

She pulled back with wide eyes. "I don't think that's a good idea."

"Shelby. You can trust me. I'm trying to help."

"And I really appreciate it. But you can't stay." Her fingertips ran back and forth through the day's stubble. "Thank you so much, Jeff."

She delicately kissed his cheek and he held on, pulling her in for a hug.

"I can stay outside," he whispered.

"That's what the police are doing."

"Then I can stay on your back porch." He smiled at her chuckle. "I'm worried."

With a heavy sigh, he stepped back, crossing her arms with a faint smile. "He took pictures, planted bugs, opened my doors, but he's not here and he's not hurting me. I don't like any of the things he's done, but after all that, he's not even approached me."

"Stalkers don't until they do, and then it's bad." He frowned. "I'm not trying to scare you, but I want you to be aware."

"He's not here."

Jeff nodded.

"Then I'll be safe tonight. You go home and sleep, and I'll try and sleep too." She shrugged. "I've run from a lot of things, Jeff. I'm not so interested in running anymore."

"You want to share?"

"I'm tired. Maybe another time."

He wrapped her up once more. It was too hard to just walk away.

"I'll be safe tonight. Let's take it one day at a time."

"You working tomorrow?"

She nodded into his chest. "At the clinic. I go in at eight and leave at five."

"Text me the address and I'll be there to follow you home."

"You're doing too much."

"Not enough."

His face heated as another kiss landed on his cheek.

"You can go now."

"You keep giving me kisses like that and I'll start thinking something else, Shelby."

She chuckled, stepping back with that amazing smile on her face. "Maybe that's something we can talk about another time too?"

"Counting on it."

Planting a kiss on her forehead, he turned and headed for the door. She closed the door with a wave, and after hearing the lock, he stepped off the porch.

"Going to be a long night," he mumbled with a deep breath, his whole body on fire at the possibility of that conversation happening sooner rather than later.

SHELBY LEANED AGAINST THE DOOR, heart pounding and tears running down her cheeks. How could something so scary and wonderful happen at the same time on the same day? As terrified as she was that some guy had decided to stalk her, the fact she was able to fall into Jeff's arms, that he wanted to be there for her, had her heart beating double-time.

God, please keep me from messing this all up.

Self-doubt, her past, all the things she'd held onto for so long would bombard her and ruin all of this in an instant. Telling Jeff what had happened was a must, but maybe after this was all over with?

Groaning, she grabbed a glass of ice water and headed for her room. Sleep would be fleeting tonight, but maybe she could hold onto the feeling of Jeff's arms around her to protect her for a little longer. At least until she could fall asleep.

"I have to sleep tonight." The thought of the clinic work, the rotation she'd picked up for a friend, and the importance of getting it all right.

God, give me peace.

24

Thursday

Jeff let out a yawn as he poured himself some coffee. No sleep, constantly checking his phone to see if Shelby texted; he was more than exhausted.

Frowning at the light filtering from under Buck's door, he glanced at the clock.

Six in the morning. Typically, Buck would be at the gym, not at his desk at this hour.

He knocked on the door to Buck's office and stepped inside. "What's going on?" He paused to see the furrowed brow on Buck's face as he looked up from behind the computer. "What'd you find?"

"I think I've figured out what Frazier was talking about." Buck motioned to the computer.

Jeff walked around the desk and studied the screen. A folder labeled "Laundry List" sat open. Lists of dates and files within the folder filled the box.

"You hacked into the police commissioner's account?" Jeff's face heated and the coffee rose in his throat. "Buck, you're going to jail."

"Technically, it's not hacking. Frazier gave me the passwords years ago when he was worried about some threats. I helped him out and when I needed answers after everything with Danica, I just checked to see if the passwords were still the same." Buck shrugged. "They still work. I missed this on the first search, but after that meeting yesterday, I wanted to see what had him so jumpy."

"He was pretty upset. I'm surprised he didn't arrest you." Jeff collapsed in the chair on the other side of the desk. "Even if he's being blackmailed by someone, what does that have to do with us? Or even Dani and Kyra?"

"First off, it is blackmail. There are different receipts over the past several years. Frazier's been commissioner for five years, and this file folder has at least that many years of information. The receipts are for dinners, lodging, plane tickets, and excursions. I've researched the dates and they don't line up to anything he'd be attending under his duty as commissioner."

"So he's skimming from the city?"

Buck nodded.

"What do you plan on doing with it?"

"Nothing." Buck leaned back in his chair. "He's up to something and this is my only leverage. If I have this, then maybe he'll talk to me."

"He said he'd throw you in jail if you came to see him again. I believe him."

"Then I won't go see him. There're other ways to get in touch."

"Ways that can be used at your trial," Jeff mumbled and took a much-needed sip of coffee. "All of this does make him look guilty, but of what? What's his motive? The men responsible for Dani are dead or in jail. The attacks on us have all but stopped. Roltz still seems to hate us for some reason, but other than that, it's been quiet. You really want to stir up trouble?"

"I don't have to stir it up. It's just not making headway at the moment."

Jeff's phone buzzed and he pulled it from his pocket, frowning at the blocked number before answering. "It's a little early in the morning for scam calls, don't you think?"

A woman's chuckle echoed on the line. "I'm looking for Buck Thompson. I was told you're the man to reach."

Jeff met Buck's stare. "Why am I the man, and who is Buck Thompson?"

"Don't play games, Mr. Powers." The sickly sweet voice made Jeff's teeth clench. "I know you're very close with him, as are Danica and Kyra Freeman. It's important I speak to him, in person."

"I'll have to see if he's available."

"Operation Luddock."

"What?"

"Just tell him that. I'll shoot you a text, let me know when he's ready to talk. Otherwise, I'll go public with just one side, and trust me, it won't be the story you're hoping for."

The call ended and Buck stood.

"Who was that?"

"Someone looking for you. She said to mention Operation Luddock."

Buck's face went crimson.

"She said she'll go public if you don't speak with her."

"I need to make a call," Buck mumbled, storming from the room.

The tide was turning and the pull in Jeff's chest told him they were once again in trouble.

God, give us strength and sound mind. He blew out a deep breath. *We're going to need it.*

JEFF SMILED at the text message as he sat at the kitchen island.

Thanks so much for all your help. It means a lot to me.

Shelby was an amazing and wonderful woman, and he was getting too close. It had been a long time since he'd even had this kind of attraction to a woman. But with their talk last night, the way she watched him, it was taking all his energy to keep from falling way too hard so soon.

Buck walked into the main room, face and neck red.

"You want to talk?"

Buck motioned to his office.

"What's going on?"

"I'll tell you later," Jeff mumbled as he walked past Danica and Haiden on the couch watching T.V. Shutting the door behind him, Jeff waited as Buck paced.

"There was a breech."

"What kind of breech? Where?"

"The kind where classified information gets downloaded and taken from a so-called secure location."

Jeff winced.

"If this woman does have information, it could take me down."

"You're saying you did something wrong?" Jeff stepped in front of Buck. "What happened?"

"Too much to explain, even if I could."

"Give me the basics."

Stepping to the desk, Buck sat on the edge, crossing his arms.

"A mission went south, we lost almost everyone."

"Everyone but you?"

Buck nodded. "There was an investigation since I was the sole survivor, and there were ... extenuating circumstances."

Jeff's heart started pounding. "Explain."

Even Buck's crippling stare and frown wouldn't work this time. "I need to know what circumstances are around you being in trouble and investigated."

"I didn't get in trouble."

"But it was investigated?"

Buck nodded.

"Well?"

With a sigh, Buck's shoulders fell. "Jeff, it was a long time ago."

"I'd like to be prepared whenever this person comes forward with whatever she has on you."

"She doesn't have all of it. It's not all in the report."

"Buck, what's going on?" Jeff had never asked many questions about Buck's service, not that he would be allowed to give up much anyway. But the defeated look on Buck's face indicated something more.

"At the time I was deployed, I was involved with a woman named Nikki. She worked at the camp, and although it was frowned upon, she wasn't Army so we weren't breaking any rules."

"I don't remember that name."

Buck chuckled. "Let's just say there are a lot of names you'd not recognize. She was a warrior. If she'd been born a man, she'd be leading the Rangers, taking point and finishing top of the class. She had a fighting spirit like I've never seen.

"When I was briefed on a situation overseas, I was told to put together a team. She was the first person I thought of. Where we were going, she spoke the language, she blended in well. Brown eyes, dark skin and black hair, her linguistics were perfect, and she could give us an edge."

Buck shook his head. "I had a lot of trouble getting her approved. Once they found out we'd been friendly, they told me no, it would be impossible for her to go. But one of my superiors knew Nikki was skilled and looked beyond the fact we'd been dating, beyond the fact she's a woman, and said it would be foolish to keep her on the bench."

"Wow. That's saying a lot."

"At the time, it was. Women in combat wasn't a thing. It wasn't encouraged and I sure got an earful by everyone that I pulled onto the mission. So, I had her credentials printed out and put into a file, her name and picture redacted. I said if she can't come, what about this one and handed it out to the others."

Jeff chuckled.

"They all said yes. It was a no-brainer. But they were sure surprised when she showed up."

"You didn't tell them?"

"Nope. Not until we were set to leave." Buck let out a sigh. "We entered the area at night. She went ahead of us, posing as a local. It wasn't long until she had us right where we were supposed to be, an hour early. She was on the inside and could feed us information. The insertion was supposed to be a twelve-hour mission. After six, it all went bad."

Buck's eyes glazed over. "In a field, we were bedded down, waiting for the information to arrive." He cut his eyes to Jeff. "We'd been there for thirty minutes and then I heard a scream. It was a woman's scream and I immediately knew someone figured her out.

"It didn't take long for the locals to enlist some help and we were bombarded with mortars, setting the field on fire and doing their best to find us. We tried to back out without being seen, but it was like a never-ending firefight."

Jeff's heart pounded.

"In every direction, my men were dying, we were being pounded on all sides. The fire broke out and I couldn't pull anyone else, I couldn't get them out." Buck cleared his throat. "After that, I somehow managed to break through, finding a grove to lay low and call it in. They sent in a backup team and we finished the mission."

"And Nikki?"

"We found her a few days later. They'd done what they could to get information from her. But we brought her home."

Barely able to speak, Jeff stood there dumbfounded, a lump in his throat.

"Because she died, the team died, it was investigated. She wasn't even supposed to be there—it wasn't like they put it all down on paper." Buck glanced up. "It was a verbal acceptance that wasn't supposed to be contested."

"So when it was contested, no one had anything to say."

Buck nodded.

"I'm sorry. I had no idea."

"I know you didn't. I intended on keeping it that way. But whoever this is, she somehow either breeched the security herself or was given the file."

"You were cleared though, right?"

"Yeah, but several people weren't happy about it. I had men that thought I'd risked her life for my own needs. But they just didn't understand. She wanted to be there. She knew what was at stake and was just as willing to die for that mission as everyone else."

"But it wasn't just another one of your men," Jeff whispered.

"No, she wasn't." Buck's tired eyes met his. "I wasn't ready for what it did to me to lose her under my watch. She was one of my team, my responsibility. It made me realize I couldn't see any woman as someone other than my team. We never talked about our relationship as anything other than the here and now. Marriage was never an option."

Buck straightened and headed for the door.

"How long were you two together?"

"Five years."

Jeff sat on the arm of the chair, staring at Buck's back as he left.

His pseudo-father had a relationship for five years with a woman that died under his watch after he selected her for a mission. He'd been carrying around that weight for no telling how long.

Pulling out his phone, Jeff stared at the message on the screen. He'd been so busy trying to keep from falling all over himself with Shelby that he didn't stop to think about the cost of not telling her he wanted more.

But how do you do that with a woman that was so willing to walk away, push away, whenever things got hard?

25

Shelby let out a groan as she sat down for the first time this morning. After little sleep and a growing knot in her stomach, she was desperate for some rest. Looking over her shoulder all day long was getting old, and the paranoia was far-reaching. Just going to the bathroom gave her anxiety.

Scanning the charts, she did her best to focus on the orders scribbled out on the page. Her beeping phone brought her out of her stupor.

Hope you're having a great day.

Smiling at Jeff's text, she took a deep breath. It was only by God's grace that she'd found someone so willing to put up with her inabilities, much less the constant drama surrounding a possible stalker.

Swallowing that terrible reminder, she texted back.

It's okay. How's yours?

Not going great. I have a meeting later, but I'll be there to walk you to your car tonight.

She heaved a sigh. Thank goodness. Walking to the car after five, even in daylight with the security guard being close by, terrified her. But if he was busy …

If you're too busy, it's fine. There's a guard on duty and I don't want you to take time from your schedule to see me.

I'll be there at five. Be careful, Shelby. I'll see you soon.

Her heart pounded.

How did she get here? Already falling for a guy she barely knew, excited at the chance to get to see him, it all seemed too much, too fast.

Lord, what am I going to do?

———

JEFF OPENED the door to a short woman with even shorter jet black hair.

"Mr. Powers?"

He nodded and motioned her inside.

"I was surprised you wanted to meet at your office. I just assumed Buck would hire an attorney."

"It was his decision," Jeff mumbled and led her to the large conference room.

Buck stood, his stare already in place.

"And this is Buck Thompson, I assume." The woman stuck out her hand and Buck just nodded. The woman's gaze went to the corner. "Who is that?"

"Evan Mitchell. He's part of our team as well."

The woman glared at Jeff. "Are you attempting to intimidate me, Mr. Powers?"

"No. If we wanted to do that, we'd be at our lawyer's office. Either you sit down with all of us here and now, or this doesn't happen."

The woman seemed thrown as her eyes darted back and forth between them.

"You've not given us your name."

"Destiny Travers. I'm an independent writer."

Buck huffed. "And how did you get this information?"

She chuckled and sat down, pulling out her phone and hitting some buttons. "First off, I don't give up sources, that's why people come to me. I never give up anyone, I've been in jail twice." Confidently grinning, she sat the phone in-between her and Buck, the recording app running. "Secondly, this meeting is only a formality so that I can post what I've already written. I'm not some one-sided reporter. I do get both sides of the story, although I'm afraid with the information I have, your words today won't measure up to a reputable explanation. I have the facts. Conclusive statements from our own government."

"How is that getting both sides of the story? You've already written and are running with the first draft, don't pretend your being here is in empathy for whatever you know." Jeff's jaw ached as he gritted out the words.

Destiny cut her eyes to him. "You're not even needed here, Mr. Powers."

"I'm not leaving. Either say your piece, or you can go."

With a shake of her head, she opened her satchel and pulled out a file. As she took the pages from the folder, she stacked them in front of her.

"Having redacted military files like that are against the law," Evan mumbled.

"It doesn't matter if it's against the law. I'm here for the truth." She slid them over to Buck, who refused to pick them up. "Operation Luddock was in June of 2002, correct?"

"No comment."

She rolled her eyes. "It was an overseas mission to collect information and in the course of that disaster, several American men and women were killed, correct?"

"No comment."

Destiny folded her hands on top of the table. "Come now, Mr. Thompson. You have something to say, don't you?"

"Why don't you tell us what you're accusing him of?" Jeff paced the room, speaking up since Buck wasn't saying a word.

"Buck Thompson was the sole survivor of what could only be described as either a complete lack of judgment or an attack from within."

Evan scoffed. "You're calling him a traitor?"

"It was investigated as such. But as usual, Uncle Sam refused to prosecute one of its own trained and decorated officers. I plan on re-opening the investigation."

"With what evidence?" Buck finally spoke up. "Do you have the entire file?"

"Of course. Even though the redacted information, which by the way, isn't exactly foolproof. I can tell exactly what happened. The investigation was a sham, none of the evidence was properly considered, and Americans died because of his reckless behavior or because of his lack of judgment."

"And you think, in all your wisdom of knowing about this for all of what, a day, is enough to change anyone's mind?" Jeff could feel the heat rising up his neck.

A miserable smile spread across her face. "All I need is public opinion, gentlemen."

"To what end?"

"To convict and prosecute Buck Thompson."

"Dr. Durning, I have a man that says you've agreed to see him?"

Shelby took a seat next to the receptionist, Debbie. "Okay, what's his name?"

"Terry Quarters?"

"What? I thought he was still in the hospital?"

"Apparently not. He said he'd be released today but wanted to set up an appointment for tomorrow."

The thought of Terry Quarters coming to see her made her stomach clench.

"Um, is there a time slot to put him?"

Debbie scrolled through the screen. "I can maybe work him in right before lunch?"

"Sounds good. Thanks."

Shelby headed for her office, heart pounding and arms shaky. That man lied to the police and refused to speak with her regarding everything that happened. But here in the office, maybe he'd open up more, explain why he asked to see her that day

Pulling up her contacts, she called Dr. William French.

It was impossible for Terry to be out so soon. He needed much more rest and probably some counseling as well.

"This is Betty."

"Hey, Betty. It's Shelby Durning."

"Oh, hi. How's things at the clinic? Better than the hospital?"

Shelby chuckled at the nurse practitioner's sarcasm. "It's wonderful here. Maybe you can join us sometime?"

"Yeah, right. I need much more excitement."

"Speaking of excitement, I just booked an appointment for one of William's patients. I thought for certain he'd still be in the hospital, but he said he's getting out today."

"Who is it?"

"Terry Quarters."

"Oh."

That tone didn't sound good.

"What's that about?"

"He's non-compliant. The guy can barely get around but he's determined to leave. William tried to get him to stay a little longer, but no luck. Why does he want to see you?"

"I'm not sure. I mean, someone might've told him what happened in the ER since he doesn't remember."

"He doesn't? I went in there earlier to try my hand at getting him to stay, and he said he didn't want the same guy that attacked him in the ER to come after him again. I think he remembers more than what he's saying."

Shelby sighed. "Well, okay."

"You still going to see him?"

"I mean, he asked for me, so yeah, I'll see him. I just hope he's willing to at least follow some orders. He could bust his stitches or worse if he's not careful."

"Good luck, Shel. You're going to need it."

"Thanks," she mumbled as she hung up the phone.

It made no sense why Terry would be so adamant about leaving the hospital. Detective Fredricks had already told Terry that his attacker was in prison. He was in no danger and needed to be monitored after what he'd been through.

"Hey Shelby, your next patient is ready."

"Thanks."

Whatever was going on with Terry Quarters would have to wait until tomorrow. Maybe then she'd get the answers needed from that terrible day.

26

Jeff glared adamantly at smug Destiny Travers.

"I'd like to hear your rebuttal." Buck crossed his arms. "I don't think you have anything of value, and you're hoping to gain intel from me."

She flipped through the pages. "This is the after-action report. Eight men were pulled from a field outside a village. Their remains were riddled with damage from weaponry and were burned beyond recognition."

Buck's jaw clenched.

"And then, there's the remains of a woman that the villagers, well, let's just say I almost lost my lunch."

"Easy." Evan bellowed.

"Like you could even imagine." Destiny stood. "What this man has done, it's inexcusable."

"It's war." Evan's arms tightened across his chest as his face turned red. "You have no idea what you're talking about."

"It wasn't war. We weren't at war with anyone at the time."

"We were, but not in that county."

"Is this funny to you?"

"Calm down." Jeff stepped in as Destiny's face turned

crimson. "No one is making jokes, and we all understand how this works. We all know much more about how horrible humans can be to other humans when they want something from them. Much more than you do."

She scoffed. "So I'm just some ignorant woman?"

"No, you're inexperienced. You've not seen what we've seen. I've investigated cases where torture is a nice word and the remains we've found couldn't even measure up. That was in the U.S., so don't make this about you versus us."

"Is that why you do what you do?" Destiny turned her attention to Buck. "If it is, do they know how much you fail?"

"Fail at what?" Buck's gravelly voice rose.

"To protect everyone around you." She produced a picture and slid it across the table. "They all died. Why didn't you?"

Jeff took a step forward and recognized Buck instantly in the photo of the small group of men. One figure stood out, partially hiding behind his shoulder. Much smaller with beautiful, large brown eyes.

Buck stood. "Have you been in war?"

"Of course not."

"Then you don't know. If you've not been there, been through what we see, what we experience, then you can't pass judgment. Post what you will, do what you want. But this won't end here. Your career won't last past those pictures."

"Is that a threat? A recorded threat?" she tapped the table next to the phone.

"I don't need to make threats. I'm just telling you the truth. That picture was taken two days before I lost my entire team. I received a new one within ten hours, and we did our job. You should learn to do yours."

Brushing past Evan, Buck left out the door.

Jeff took off after Buck, stepping outside in the cool air. Screeching tires and the discharge of gunfire erupted and he dove for cover. A black mustang sped by, spraying the outside of the building and narrowly missing his head as he huddled on the ground behind some trash bins.

"Buck!" Jeff jumped up and sprinted around the corner as the car sped away.

"I'm good." Buck rolled over and looked up at him from the sidewalk. "Get the plates?"

Jeff extended his hand and helped Buck to stand.

"Echo Romeo six two three," Evan answered as he stood behind them. "Based on the way they tried to hide the plate, my guess is stolen."

"Then it's been stolen for a few days."

Jeff huffed. "It's the same one from the diner and from the hospital. I need to call Fredricks."

Buck nodded as sirens sounded in the distance. "I think the reporter in there has some questions to answer. If she was given that material, maybe she's the link to whoever is coming after us."

PACING, Jeff kept an eye on his phone for the time. He didn't want to be late getting to the clinic to walk Shelby to her car.

"She's not talking." Detective Marty DeSalis appeared from the office. "She just keeps raving about her rights and some nonsense about police brutality."

"I pulled the video from the outside of the office. The Mustang pulled in a few minutes after she arrived and parked." Buck handed DeSalis the flash drive. "You might consider holding her for a bit, I have a feeling someone else will want a word."

Marty frowned. "And why was she here?"

"Interview." Jeff continued to pace.

"What happened?" Danica rushed inside, Haiden on her heels.

"Someone is targeting us again," Buck answered. "This time, it's me."

"I think it's all of us." Jeff turned to Marty. "You need to get in touch with Detective Fredricks. The same black Mustang is being investigated for a possible stalker attempt on Shelby Durning."

"It's the same car?" Dani's jaw dropped.

"Yeah, we ID'd the driver, but she's never seen him before. He slipped some pictures under her hotel door. I was hoping Fredricks would have a line on him by now."

"Maybe it was an attack on you, then, for stepping in." Haiden's slow drawl made sense.

"Could be, hadn't thought of that."

Marty nodded. "I'll look into it and let you know. We'll go ahead and take her to the station, wait for whatever call is coming in. If she does give us something, I'll let you know."

"Thanks, Marty." Jeff watched as the officers escorted the red-faced Destiny out the door. "You know, I think Haiden's on to something. We've got two separate cases, just like when Dani went missing."

"*Went* missing?" Danica muttered.

Haiden wrapped an arm around her waist.

"Explain."

Jeff looked to Buck. "I saw the same car at Shelby's house after the gas incident. It was leaving and followed her down the road. I didn't think anything of it. Then I saw it again at the diner."

"I remember."

"Then, it appears on the hotel security video where Shelby stayed. Maybe he's after me, too, for being too close to Shelby. If he gets jealous, it could escalate things."

"I think she needs to come here," Evan muttered.

"I agree."

Jeff nodded at Danica. "I can ask, but she's not interested in being protected. She's more than concerned her reputation would be ruined if she ends up in protective custody. I've already tried."

"I'm sure you did." Danica cracked a smile. "But if you explain what could happen, not to scare her, but just to let her know the danger, she might be understanding. There's no way she sees just how bad this is all unraveling."

Jeff sighed. "Yeah, she mentioned not being worried that the guy hasn't been physical. I hope it doesn't get to that point."

Buck's phone went off. "I have to take this."

Watching Buck walk away, Jeff's mind raced.

"What's going on? You didn't fill me in this morning." Danica crossed her arms. "He's acting ... off."

"A reporter showed up asking about a certain incident. Buck was investigated and cleared, but she's out for blood. Already has a write-up ready to publish depicting Buck as a traitor that killed Americans."

"What?" Haiden's curt tone covered Danica's gasp.

"I know." Jeff shook his head. "We were meeting with her when Buck left. I followed, and then a black Mustang came barreling down the road, taking shots."

"But the story, is she going to publish it?"

Jeff shrugged at Dani. "Don't know. But her info corresponds with a breech of security, and that same information was hacked from a server. I'm assuming she can either go to jail or give up her source."

"She was adamant that wouldn't happen." Evan sighed. "But still, her coming after Buck specifically. Then suggesting public opinion is all that's needed? Someone with some major hacking skills got her that file just to ruin us."

"Could be anyone we've helped to put away," Haiden mumbled.

"Or someone that's still in the wind?" Evan set his gaze on Jeff.

"I don't know," Jeff shrugged. "You'll have to ask Buck about that one. I've got to go. See you later. Call if you find anything else out."

As much as he didn't want to leave, he needed to be there for Shelby. And for the first time in his life, he'd much rather spend time with a beautiful woman than be at work, trying to break down a criminal's mind.

27

Shelby could see the strain behind Jeff's smile as he walked into the lobby. "Sorry I'm a little late."

"You're not late. I finished early." She stood and pocketed her cell phone. "Is everything all right?"

Jeff shrugged. "Not really. Have you heard from Detective Fredricks?"

Her heart dropped to her stomach. "No, why?"

"I think things are escalating."

"What things?" she whispered.

Jeff looked around the lobby and took hold of her elbow. "Let's talk at your house."

As he led her to the parking lot, her pulse quickened. His head on a swivel, he didn't say a word, just kept her pulled in tight.

"Jeff, you're worrying me. What's happened?"

He hit the button on her doorhandle. "I'll explain at your house, okay?" He ushered her into the vehicle. "I'll be right behind you. You're fine. I promise."

Stifling the urge to disagree, she nodded, and he slammed her door shut.

God, give me some courage.

After an excruciating twenty-minute drive home, she opened the garage door and slowly pulled inside. Jeff was at her door before she could gather her purse, opening it for her.

"Thanks," she mumbled.

Once inside, she sat down her things and leaned against the counter. "Okay, what's got you so paranoid?"

"The black Mustang appeared again. This time, he unloaded on our office."

"What? Unloaded, what does that mean?"

Jeff narrowed his eyes as bile built up in her throat.

"He ... he shot at you? Was anyone hurt?"

"No, we're all fine. But it does mean he's escalating."

Holding her chest, she sat on the barstool. "Escalating?"

Jeff sat down, taking her hand in his. "I'm not trying to scare you, Shelby. I just want you to understand what he's capable of. I think he sees me as competition and someone to get rid of to get to you. This time, he used a gun to try and make his point."

"Then ... then you should go." She stood, pulling her hand from his. "I mean, I don't want something to happen to you because of me."

"Shelby."

"Jeff, seriously." Swallowing the need for a breakdown, she attempted to control the hysterics building in her voice. "I ... I appreciate you trying to help me. But I think Detective Fredricks was right. This is too dangerous, and I'm just putting you in more danger than necessary."

He took hold of her elbows and gently pulled her in. Wrapping her arms around him, she held on tight, losing the little bit of composure she'd managed to keep all day.

"I'm not leaving, and I'm thinking you should come stay at our office until he's caught."

"But then your office will be the target," she mumbled into his chest.

"Then I'm staying here."

She pulled back to see the smile on his face. "Jeff, you can't be serious."

"I am. There are no officers outside your house. I'm sure they were pulled. So either I'm staying inside or outside. Your choice."

Dumfounded, she stepped back, unsure what to say.

"How about we order some food, and then maybe you can decide before it gets too late." With a wink, he pulled out his phone and settled on her couch, his thumb scrolling through the screen.

"Wait—I mean—" Struggling to finish a thought, she sat once more on the stool. "Why hasn't Detective Fredricks found him yet? He has the guy's picture. And if he's connected to me, it can't be that hard. It's not like I know that many people."

"I agree." Jeff leaned in on his knees. "So, how about we order some food and go through all the guys you know. It might help out."

She frowned at the grin on his face. "You're just being nosy and want to ask embarrassing questions."

He chuckled. "I'm not denying how amusing I'm anticipating the conversation will be, but it's not the only reason."

With a sigh, she stood. "I'm going to go change."

"What do you want me to order?"

"Some good Thai food. I've not found a good place yet."

"That I can do."

"And no snooping, remember?"

"I'll do my best."

Attempting to refrain from smiling at that great smile and wink, she turned and headed to her bedroom.

How in the world was he able to do that? All the fear and worry just disappeared and left her with nothing but a need to sit on the couch with him, letting him take it all away.

"Get yourself together."

She needed a shower and a new plan. Jeff was an amazing guy that said and did all the right things. It was getting easier and easier to just let him in, let him take over the situation. But he didn't know all of it, all the misdeeds of her life. Once he did, would he see her for the failure everyone else did?

Groaning, she turned on the water and stepped into the warm stream.

"God, just wash this all away. Please."

WATCHING T.V. WITH JEFF, Shelby jumped at the sound of her phone vibrating.

"Hello?"

"Hey, Dr. Durning. It's Detective Fredricks. Do you recognize the name Bruce Morrison?"

She sat up, Jeff pulling the receiver down to listen. "No, I don't recognize that name. Who is he?"

"The man in the mustang that delivered the pictures. He's a small-time felon, nothing that would necessarily insinuate stalker behavior."

"I don't recognize the name at all."

"Okay, then. Just thought I'd check. I will have an officer there shortly. We've had a few call in, so we've been short-handed tonight. Someone should be there by eleven and will stay all night. They'll keep an eye out for you."

"Thanks, I appreciate that."

"Let me know if anything else comes up."

"I will." As she ended the call, she leaned her head against Jeff's. "Well, I guess that solves one problem."

"Problem? I'm a problem?"

She chuckled. "Not a problem. I'm sorry, I misspoke." Making the mistake of looking up, she paused at his bright blue eyes staring into hers, inches away. "I meant to say, I'm glad I don't have to make that decision."

Jeff's thumb trailed her jaw, easing her closer. His eyes darting back and forth, he gave her a gentle kiss.

"Probably for the best," he whispered.

Heart pounding, she leaned in again, receiving a wonderful, toe-curling kiss.

"I ..." she took a breath as Jeff gave her a grin.

"Don't take it back now, Shelby."

"I wasn't going to."

His eyes narrowed. "I'm not asking. Okay? Even now, after that, I'm not asking for you to tell me anything. We both have things to talk about, we both have a past. But that doesn't mean it has to be right now."

Swallowing hard, she gave a nod.

"I'll stay until the officer arrives, then I'll head back to the office. Unless you've changed your mind about me staying here?"

She frowned. "Jeff."

"Just thought I'd ask." He let out a chuckle and pulled her in for a hug.

Leaned back in the couch, wrapped up in Jeff's arms, she knew she was in trouble. There was no more worry about falling too far or giving in too soon. She was already way over her head in love with Jeff Powers.

28

Friday

Jeff strode into the police station, hoping for some good news. It'd been hard enough last night to walk out of Shelby's house with just a quick hug and kiss. But not knowing where the stalker Bruce Morrison was had kept him up all night.

"Detective."

Fredricks only frowned up at him. "Powers. What brings you by?"

"Just wanting some answers on that black Mustang. If you've got them." Ignoring Fredricks' glare, Jeff sat on the edge of the desk.

"The vehicle is registered to a Kaci White, deceased. The tags are still in her name, but with no family, we're trying to track down where her personal belongings were sent."

"Probably an auction."

"My guess too. And before you ask, no hits on Bruce Morison. I've put out a BOLO, we'll see if we can get lucky. I talked to Detective DeSalis this morning as well. He said you had an interesting afternoon."

Jeff's face heated. "Sure, let's go with interesting."

"I'm not sure we're going to have luck with that car, but I do have an alert for any black Mustang to be stopped and checked out. However, we've got more important things to do this morning." Fredricks clipped on his gun. "He wants you."

"Who?"

"Goodwin. He only wants to talk to you."

"When?"

Fredricks pulled his jacket on. "Let's go."

Riding in the cruiser with the detective, Jeff finally broke the uncomfortable silence. "What changed your mind about me being involved?" Jeff watched as Fredricks frowned.

"I finally got the video."

"You saw something?"

"Terry approaches Randal. They talk, then they both react at the same time. It was so quick, I couldn't even tell what happened."

"A friend of mind mentioned that sometimes, a switch flips in that kind of situation. Protection. My friend mentioned Randal might've been trying to protect the girl."

Fredricks slowly nodded. "So you think once he disarmed Terry, he was trying to keep the girl from further injury?"

"I think so. Randal is reacting to an attack and slips into protection mode. She was the youngest person there and was close enough she couldn't get away from the chaos."

"I have to give the DA a recommendation."

"By when?"

Fredricks glanced over. "Tomorrow."

"What's the family say?"

"They're mad. They have a right to be."

Jeff nodded and stared out the window. "If we can make the connection, maybe we can convince them he was trying to protect her."

"Not sure that'll be enough. Media like it is, they've already portrayed him as an attacker, dangerous. Even with a recommendation to not charge him, I can't guarantee the DA won't move forward."

"Then we need him talking," Jeff mumbled as they pulled into the parking lot.

Following Fredricks into the visitor's area, Jeff paced the room.

"Just so you know, it's nothing against you."

"What's against me?"

"Talking about a dirty cop is still talking about a cop, and it's hard news to swallow."

Jeff paused a moment, the memory of a few months ago flashing through his mind. Detective Barry Sullivan, AKA Oscar Burnett. "But we didn't. We never even gave a report about what happened to anyone but the commissioner."

"Your boss did."

"What? When?"

"It was all over the local online news. The entire statement, from Buck Thompson. It was a huge slander against the police department and one that no one is going to forget anytime soon."

Jeff stood there slack-jawed. "Wait a second. We never spoke to the media about what happened. None of us did. Buck would be the last person to do that, he's been trying hard to get this thing all cleaned up."

"Don't know what to tell you. It's all there, and it's bad. You can look it up for yourself." Fredricks shrugged as they were led into the holding room.

Randal was escorted in and sat at the table as they started to handcuff his wrists to the metal loop.

"That's not necessary," Fredricks said as he sat opposite Randal.

"Thanks." Randal nodded to Fredricks and looked up at him. "Glad you could make it."

"I was told you wanted to speak with me."

Randal let out a breath. "I want to talk about what happened, clear my name. I've been thinking over and over again, trying to remember what went down." He shook his head. "It's in there, I just can't find all of it. But I know—I know I didn't *want* to hurt anyone."

"I think this will help." Jeff pulled out his phone and a picture of Terry. "You know this man?" He sat the phone down in front of Fredricks so Randal could see it.

"Yeah, that's Payday. He's ..." Randal's eyes widened, then he blinked a few times. "I remember," he whispered.

"Tell me." Fredricks turned on his phone to record. "Or do you want to wait for counsel?"

"No. I want to tell you what happened. Myles, he called and said he was real sick. He wanted me to meet him at the ER in case he needed someone there to help him home. I walked inside to wait. After a while, Payday came up and sat next to me. He said I needed to go."

"He asked you to leave?"

Looking up at Fredricks, Randal nodded. "Guy's a jerk, might be a troublemaker, but he's harmless. That's when I noticed the knife. The butt was sticking out the top of his boot, and I asked why he had it. Payday said he had a job to do and if I didn't leave, he'd make me. I told him he should try." Randal blew out a breath. "He tried."

"And the girl?"

Randal's jaw tensed at Fredrick's question.

"Randal?" Jeff pushed.

"When Payday walked over, he sat between me and her. She screamed. After that ..." He shook his head. "I don't know what his plan was, but he was going to make a scene. I did what I could, but honestly, I don't even remember having a hold of her. I thought she was behind me."

Jeff snatched his phone and called for the guard.

Fredricks stood. "What?"

"Shelby. Terry asked to see Shelby. That means there's something else going on and she's in the middle of it."

"You think Terry and Dierks were on the same side? Going after her for some reason?"

"I don't know, but I need to find out."

"Please see to it that his insurance is billed correctly and mail any correspondence. He says he doesn't use email."

"Yes, ma'am."

Shelby nodded to Debbie as she walked from the front of the office to her own.

"You have a call."

"Thanks." As she stepped into the office, her phone flashed. "Hello?"

"Dr. Durning?"

She frowned at the woman's voice. "Yes. Who's this?"

"I'm calling to discuss a situation."

"I'm sorry, who is this?"

"Are you still married to Ryan?"

Her mouth dropped as her heart pounded. "I've never been married to anyone. You have the wrong number." She hung up as her stomach clenched. Who was out there telling lies? Her cell phone vibrated. "Hello?"

"We know who you are and where you are."

Hitting the end button, she stood and nervously paced the office. Was it the reporter from the other day? Maybe so, she couldn't remember the sound of her voice. It couldn't be Ryan. He was still in Florida, and there was no way he was out and all the way here.

Screams shattered her thoughts and she sprinted down the hallway filling with smoke.

"Get out! Everyone out!" Shelby assisted a few of the older patients into the waiting area as the nurses helped to lead them down the stairwell.

"Shelby?"

She turned and gasped at the gun pointing right at her.

29

"Mr. Quarters?" Shelby did her best to remain calm as the man held one of the nurses by the throat, but the gun was aimed at her.

"You have to come with me."

"I don't know what you mean. Come with you? Where?" Gripping her hands in front of her, she attempted to calm the shaking.

"He'll kill me if you don't."

Before she could get another word out, the nurse turned in one swift move and put the man on the floor, twisting his wrist until the gun dropped. But not before it went off, shattering the glass doors behind Shelby.

With a scream, Shelby ducked down, cowering against the wall as several uniformed police officers rushed inside. Terry Quarters lay writhing on the floor, a bloody lip and nose as he wailed.

"He threatened Dr. Durning."

Staring in shock at the nurse, Shelby was speechless as the police entered.

"Come on."

Shelby took the nurse's hand. "I'm sorry, I'm new here. What's your name?"

"Freeda. I'm sorry it took me so long to disarm him. I needed him distracted."

"How are you ... why're you so calm?"

The woman shrugged. "I was a corpsman in the Marines. That guy wasn't very strong. Why did he want you?"

Her body shaking, Shelby sat down on one of the chairs in the waiting room. "I have no idea," she whispered.

"Let me get you some water."

Staring at the chaotic scene in front of her, Shelby couldn't even hear the voices, the rattle of the gurney as Terry Quarters was taken away. A bloody stain once again on the floor from the same man as the ER incident.

"Shelby?" Jeff's voice echoed and he rushed through the room, collapsing at her feet.

"Jeff? How did you—"

"Are you okay?"

"Yes, I'm just a little shook up. How did you get here so fast?"

"I was on my way. I think Terry Quarters was planning something."

"He did."

"Quarters did this?"

She nodded as his face went red. "Why? How did you know?"

"Come on," he mumbled and took her arm to help her stand. "Detective Fredricks needs a word."

Swallowing the need to vomit, she leaned against Jeff as she stood.

"Let's talk in your office." Detective Fredricks appeared, motioning her past the bloody stain and down the hallway.

"Where's the fire? I remember smelling smoke." She sat in her office chair, leaning her elbows on the desk as she held her hair back.

"There was a small fire in the waiting area. Quarters wanted to clear the room so that you and the nurse were all that was left."

"But why?"

"That's what I want to know." The detective stared her down from the other side of the desk.

"I have no idea."

"The nurse said he wanted to take you somewhere, and he would be killed if you didn't come."

She shook her head, mouth hanging open.

"Dr. Durning, I need an answer here."

"I have no idea why he wanted to take me or where." She glanced up at Jeff, feeling the heat rising on her cheeks.

"We just learned that Terry Quarters, the man you saved, was in the ER that day to attack you with a knife. The same one Randal Goodwin used to protect himself."

"What?" she gasped.

"Randal Goodwin stepped in, and when you saved Terry's life, Dierks Carver came in to make sure he didn't talk. You're at the center of this whether you want to believe it or not."

"But I—I have no idea. You have to believe me." Her hands fisted.

"I have to ask again. Have you been in contact with Ryan Cushing?"

"No." Her jaw clenched, her eyes refusing to look up at Jeff.

Fredricks motioned to Jeff. "Can you guys give me a second?"

Her eyes widened as Jeff and the other detective left the office. Jeff's backward glance was the last thing she saw as the door closed.

"Dr. Durning, Ryan Cushing got out a month ago."

Her jaw dropped. "What?"

"You didn't know?"

Swallowing the bile burning the back of her throat, she tried to take a breath. "I had no idea. He had a sentence of a minimum of ten years."

Fredricks shrugged. "I don't know, but after getting in touch with the parole officer, he said Cushing hasn't missed an appointment."

"I don't understand. So he's still in Florida?"

"Appears to be. But this all seems very coincidental."

Gripping her arms across her chest, she did her best to keep from completely falling apart.

"Dr. Durning, what does Jeff Powers say about your situation?"

Her eyes jumped to his. "Jeff? What does he have to do with this?"

"I just wondered if you've discussed it with him. He's former law enforcement, he'd be the person to ask. I can assure you, he'd come to the same conclusion we are. This has to be one of the men or women belonging to the con job four years ago."

"Terry Quarters wasn't involved in any of that. I've never heard his name or met him before. I remember all of them. Is he connected somehow?"

Fredricks watched her for a moment. "I'll be speaking with Mr. Quarters about a lot of things. In the meantime, you might want to find a safe place until we cinch this up."

"But, if it was Terry—"

"It wasn't him at your house. He couldn't turn on the gas or plant the camera and listening devices while lying unconscious in the hospital."

She stared blankly at the wall. "You know for certain Ryan is still—he's still in Florida?"

"His parole officer sees him twice a week and keeps tabs on his job. He misses a day at work and he's in trouble so I don't see how Cushing could make it to Florida and back without missing work or meetings. But I will be following up."

Leaning back, she held her head. Her world was crumbling again, and she had yet to tell Jeff any of it. What if he decided she was completely incompetent? Or worse, wanted nothing to do with someone so easily manipulated?

"So Terry Quarters became your patient?"

Shelby nodded. "He asked if I could be his doctor and I agreed. I thought maybe he would finally tell me why he requested to see me that day in the ER. You know, since he didn't want to talk while in the hospital. But today was our first appointment and he didn't even really speak to me. I checked his stitches and that's all."

"How was he released? You told me a week minimum."

She shrugged. "He wasn't my patient while in the hospital. I spoke to his attending and Terry left against medical advice."

Fredricks stood. "Just so you know, I'm going to request you stay away from the hospital and the clinic until we know what's going on. You're making a target of anyone you come into contact with. You should remember that."

Her jaw dropped.

"That goes for Jeff Powers as well. I know he's a friend, but you're just putting him and his team in harm's way." He leaned into the desk, lording over her. "I will figure out what's going on one way or another. If you need to come clean, now is the time to do it."

She stood, shoving the chair to the wall. "I'm not involved," she hissed. "I have no idea what's going on, and for you to assert otherwise without proof is absurd. I would never endanger anyone else's life. I'm here to save lives, not take them."

Rushing from the room, her ears and face burned as she sprinted from the clinic and down the back steps. Stepping outside, the crisp air filled her burning lungs.

It was all falling apart. The new life she created, her job, and her relationship with Jeff. As much as she wanted to tell him about her past, the fear of Jeff finding her weak or stupid prodded her brain. He wouldn't be the first person to abandon her after finding out the truth.

She was here to help people; that was all God had ever led her to do. And now, she was desperate to find someone that could help her.

God, give me something.

Crossing the street to the parking lot, a screech of tires echoed.

"Shelby!"

The weight of his body slammed her to the ground as they rolled. Jeff's cologne overwhelmed her senses as she ended up on top of him.

"You okay?" Jeff gently rolled her off as she held her face. "Shelby?"

"No," she whispered, sobbing into her hands.

30

______

"What happened?"

Jeff glared at Fredricks as he carried Shelby back into the clinic. "A truck tried to run her over. When I pulled her out of the way, I think a few stitches ripped."

"I'm okay," she mumbled.

He sat her down in one of the rooms as a nurse entered.

"Let me take a quick look."

Shelby's eyes darted from the nurse to his. "Um, okay."

"I'll be outside when you're ready to go." Jeff nodded and closed the door.

"Get a look at the truck?"

Jeff shook his head at Fredricks. "Green, older model Ford. I didn't get a good look. But I bet this place has cameras."

"We're on it."

"Look, I know you don't think highly of me or my boss."

"Just your boss."

"Just so you know, he's practically my father," he hissed. "So if you don't like him, you won't like me."

Fredricks frowned.

"Whatever is going on with her or with him, it doesn't

181

matter. Someone has hired Terry to harass her and kidnap her. It's your job to figure out who."

"I know my job."

"Fredricks."

Jeff barely glanced up as the other detective came rushing up, leaning in and speaking low to Fredricks. "What's going on?"

"You've got to be kidding." Fredricks took the phone and hurried off.

"What?" Jeff turned his attention to Detective Alton.

"Terry Quarters somehow managed to get them to pull over the ambulance and he escaped."

"Escaped?"

"Not far. A dark model sedan ran him over. They just pronounced him."

Jeff's heart dropped to his stomach.

"Looks like we won't be able to question your guy. That doctor needs to figure out who wants her so bad."

"Dark model sedan? You get a make?"

Detective Alton shrugged. "Not yet. Hopefully we'll get some video."

Jeff leaned against the wall as the chaos in the office started to die down.

Who would hire Terry Quarters to kidnap Shelby?

Although certain there was much more going on from her past, including whoever Ryan Cushing was, Shelby was adamant she had no idea who could be attacking her. It would be hard to fake any of this, and now Quarters coming after her too?

The sedan was the key. If it was the same car, it connected to Shelby and the attack from yesterday at the office. But if it were about a stalker, then why send a very weak Terry Quarters to kidnap her? Had this all started when Terry came into the ER to see her?

If Terry was another pawn in this game, then someone else was ordering the moves. He was the link to the man behind this entire situation.

ONCE IN THE car with Shelby, Jeff did his best to stay calm. He needed more information about Quarters and the private conversation with Detective Fredricks.

"I didn't recognize the truck."

He snapped his gaze to her for a moment. "What?"

"The truck. It was green, but I didn't get a good look."

"I'm more concerned about the man that tried to kidnap you, Shelby." He swallowed hard at the sound of her sniffling.

"He had a gun, and the nurse ... she knocked him down, made him drop the gun."

He slammed on his brakes at the red light and turned to face her. "Why was he at your office?"

She wiped her face.

"Shelby, tell me you didn't take him on as a patient."

Her glare cut through the tears. "Don't you dare try and tell me what to do. He asked if I would treat him. I agreed. I was hoping he'd tell me why he was in the ER that day. In case you've forgotten, I've been through a lot to make sure that man lived."

"I haven't forgotten," Jeff gritted through his teeth. Staring ahead, he eased through the light.

"I'm sorry, but I'm not allowed to discuss my patients with you. I mean, I'm here to help people and if he asked to see me, I thought maybe I could figure out why."

"Did he tell you anything?"

She shook her head, digging through her purse before producing a tissue.

He snatched her hand up. "What did Fredricks say when I left?" At her silence, he noticed tears streaming down her cheek. "Shelby?"

"He keeps saying I'm in on it or that I know what's going on," she whispered.

Squeezing her hand, his frustration eased. She was just as confused as he was about what was happening.

Her phone vibrated.

"Hello?" She let out a sniffle. "I understand. I'm sorry all this—"

He frowned as she pulled her hand away, holding her head instead.

"Yes, sir. I'll be sure and let you know." She set the phone in her lap.

"Who was that?"

"My boss. He's unsure about my staying with the group at the clinic. Until the police can give him a detailed report of what happened and whose fault it is, he wants to keep the option open."

"I'm sorry, Shelby."

"Thanks," she whispered.

"You want to tell me about that man Fredricks is asking you about?"

She shook her head, pushing herself up against the door. His heart clenched. Whoever the man was, he'd done something terrible to her.

Silence spread until they reached the office. Reaching across the console, he took her hand once more. "We'll figure this out. Okay?"

Her puffy red eyes looked up at him. "You don't think it's my fault?"

"If you knew exactly who was doing this, I know you'd tell the police. And I know you wouldn't want anyone else in danger."

"Fredricks said I was putting you in danger," she whispered.

His jaw clenched. "You're not putting us in danger. We're pretty good about protection. Don't worry about us."

Her eyes studied his a moment, that same look she pinned on him the very first time he drove her home.

"What do you want, Shelby? Just ask."

She blinked a few times and disengaged, pulling her hand from his. "I'm just tired," she mumbled and opened her door.

He slid from the seat, walking to her side. Taking her elbow as she stepped down with a grimace, he pulled her in.

"Stitches?"

"A few came out. She stapled them, so they're really sore."

He slammed the door and wrapped her in a hug. "I'm sorry, Shelby. I should've been more careful."

"I was about to get hit. I think you did good."

He chuckled and squeezed her shoulders. "Good."

"Thanks for getting there so quick. Again."

"You know I've got a great response time."

She pushed out a chuckle.

In silence, he held her in the garage, letting her lean on him, her arms wrapped around his waist. If she wanted to stand here all day, he'd do it. At this point, he'd do anything to make her feel safe, protected, and loved.

Swallowing hard at the implication, he gave her a gentle kiss on the cheek.

Yeah, it was pounding in his heart. He loved Shelby, more than he could even understand.

31

"I need to go get some things if I'm going to stay here."

"Danica went to your house and packed your things."

Shelby shook her head and stepped back with a grunt. "I just started that job. It was supposed to be my opportunity to get into a medical practice once the contract with the hospital was over. Now, with all this, the attack and my inability to be at work," she swallowed. "I'm afraid if they find out I'm under protective custody they'll assume I'm at fault."

"You're being targeted. It has nothing to do with you."

Ignoring his comment, she turned and walked through the door into the office.

"Hey. Are you okay?"

Jeff stood back as Danica and Bexley took hold of Shelby and led her into the living room, taking her coat and purse from her arms.

"I'm fine. Really. It's okay."

"I'm so glad you decided to go ahead and come stay with us." Danica commented.

"Not sure I had much choice," she mumbled.

Rolling his head, he released a pop in his neck and headed for the kitchen.

"That well, huh?"

He glared at Evan and leaned back against the counter with a bottle of water.

"Can I have a word?"

Buck's voice floated from the living room and Jeff turned as Buck escorted Shelby into his office.

"I'm guessing it was a rough ride?"

Jeff frowned at Danica as she sat down on the barstool. "She's upset about her new job finding out she's now in protective custody. They've already called and said they want to keep their options open until they figure out what's going on."

"But they have to see it's not her fault. She's being targeted." Bexley slid onto a stool next to Danica.

"Doesn't matter. We all know appearances mean much more. The hospital thing, it was wrong place, wrong time. But this— this is a direct attack on her, for some reason, and in the clinic." Evan commented.

Danica crossed her arms. "Do you know what happened?"

"A patient from a previous situation took a nurse hostage and threatened to kidnap Shelby."

"That Quarters guy?"

He eyed Danica. "Then, as she was leaving, a truck tried to run her over. I got to her just in time."

"And you're certain she has no idea what's going on?"

Jeff glared at Haiden and his question.

Danica walked over to Haiden. "I think that's a valid question. Why in the world would Terry want to kidnap the woman that saved his life? Then someone else completely different run her over?"

"I've not been filled in by the detective," Jeff mumbled.

Staring at the door to Buck's office, Jeff's mind was already working overtime on whatever she couldn't bring herself to say in the car. There was something much more going on, and he was still in the dark.

Why wouldn't she just tell him who Ryan Cushing was?

Evan leaned on the island. "I'm guessing you didn't ask?"

Jeff shook his head.

"Then you need to wait her out. She needs to feel safe enough to tell you on her own." Bexley crossed her arms.

"Jeff's saved her life a few times now. What else can he do?" Evan turned to Bexley. "I'm sorry, man. Sounds like she's not looking to move forward."

"Like you would know," Danica said from behind him, and Haiden stifled a chuckle. "How did you get there so fast?"

"Fredricks and I were talking to Randal at the prison. When I showed him the picture, he knew Terry and remembered. Terry told Randal to leave, that he had business to do. Randal said he wasn't leaving. Then Terry apparently tried to make him leave."

"Business? As in Shelby?" Bexley's eyes went wide.

"It appears so, seeing how he attacked a nurse and tried to kidnap Shelby."

"He's in custody now, right? They should be able to get something from him," Evan mumbled.

"He's dead."

"What?" Danica pulled his arm and turned him toward her. "How?"

"I was there when they told Fredricks. For some reason, they pulled over the ambulance, and Terry made a run for it. He was hit by a car and died at the scene."

"It's more than just her."

Jeff stared at the Quiet Man straightening from the counter.

"One attack is an attack. Two attacks on the same person by the same assailant, even if he didn't succeed the first time, that's a planned assassination."

"But Terry didn't say he was there to kill her in the ER, did he?" Danica turned from Haiden to Jeff.

"No. Just that he had business. Randal seemed to think he was there to cause a scene. But I haven't told Shelby, so don't mention it to her. She's had a rough enough day. I tore some of her stitches when I tackled her out of the way. They had to put in staples."

Bexley winced and leaned against Evan. "Is she staying with us?"

"I'm hopeful she will. She might need some convincing."

"Then I'm in. This is my wheelhouse." Bexley winked and stood. "I'll get a schedule together, and we'll go over it once she comes out. What's Buck talking to her about anyway?"

Jeff shook his head.

Although he figured Buck knew much more about Shelby's situation than she'd told him, he had no idea what it could be. But he would be doing a search on Ryan Cushing and who he would be associated with in this area. He didn't want to dig deep enough to find out the relationship with Shelby, but he wasn't going in blind.

Besides, if Fredricks had mentioned it, then he was the problem. But if Fredricks had a name, why hadn't he done anything about him?

32

Shelby sat across from Buck, her fingers aching as she clenched them in her lap. He sat down and leaned on the desktop.

"You want to tell me, or do you want me to ask?"

"I don't have anything to say about all this. I keep telling everyone that I don't know what's going on, and I don't."

"I think you know more than what you want to admit."

"I know my past situations have nothing to do with this," she snapped.

"How can you know for sure?"

"For starters, the detective just told me that those involved," she cleared her throat. "The man involved previously is still in Florida, according to his parole officer."

"That doesn't mean his contacts are done with you."

"They're all in prison."

Buck leaned back in his chair, glaring her down. Jeff had the same glare, and even knowing they weren't actually blood-related, Jeff had obviously learned from the best.

"I'm guessing you haven't told Jeff."

"No."

"Why not?"

"Not that it's any of your business, but I'm not ready to discuss that yet." She let out a sigh. "Buck, I have great respect for you and the connection you have with Jeff. I would never hide something like this if I thought it was related. I'm a private person, and there are things Jeff hasn't shared either. I respect his decision and I know he respects mine. Four years ago ruined my life. I'm trying to keep that from happening now."

"He needs to be aware. Jeff's a smart guy and can see things you don't. That's how he was trained. It would be smart of you to let him know so he can help to keep you safe."

She mulled the comment a moment.

"And no, I'm not going to tell him. It's your story to tell, not mine. But I will remind you that he's brought you here, to his family, for protection. I will do what I need to in order to protect my people as well as you."

"I can leave if you want me to."

"No, I don't want you to. Someone has it out for you, and if they can't get Terry Quarters to talk, then it's too dangerous to go back to your home."

Leaning an elbow on the arm of the chair, she shook her head. "If I even had an idea who was doing this, I would tell you. You have to believe me. I don't want anyone in danger because of me."

Buck stood and walked around the desk, taking the seat next to her. "I believe you. If you think the other situation is over, then fine. Jeff wants you safe, and we'll do our best to keep you protected."

"Thanks, Buck." She wiped her cheeks. "I appreciate all you and the team have done to help me."

Buck stood. "You can thank Jeff. Digging into all this, what's going on with you and Randal Goodwin, wasn't in my plan. I'm trying to make peace with the police and he's been pushing. But it turns out he was right."

"I'm not sure I should be happy about that," she mumbled and stood, taking in a quick breath.

"Let's get you some ice."

Following Buck from the office, everyone turned as she paused.

"The good doctor needs some ice."

"I'll get it." Danica gave her a wink and went to the freezer.

"You can bunk with me and Danica. I've already put your stuff in our room." The pretty redhead, Bexley, gave a smile.

"Oh, I don't want to be a bother. I really appreciate everything y'all are doing. Thank you."

"It's not a bother."

She caught Jeff's blue eyes. "You want to introduce me to everyone?"

"Sorry," he chuckled. "You know Danica and Buck. This is Bexley and Evan and this is Haiden."

She nodded to each. "Um, can I ask who helped me at the hospital?"

No one spoke, but Bexley and Jeff turned to Haiden.

"Thank you for saving my life. I ... I really didn't think I would walk out of there," she whispered.

Haiden only nodded, walking past Danica and squeezing her arm. "Come on. Have a seat on the couch and get some rest. I know you're exhausted."

She followed Danica to the couch. "That's a beautiful ring. Congratulations."

Danica turned red. "Thanks."

"You and Haiden?"

Danica nodded.

Shelby eased to the couch, letting out a sigh as she fitted the ice pack to her lower back. Taking a deep breath, she closed her eyes a moment. The couch dipped and Jeff's familiar cologne floated around her.

"You need anything else?"

"No, thanks," she whispered.

He pulled at her elbow. "Shelby, it's going to be okay."

Shaking her head, she leaned over as Jeff's arm went around her, pulling her in.

"Just get some rest. I've got first shift."

She looked up. "What?"

"Fun fact, Bexley used to be in protective services. Consider yourself fully protected."

"I guess that's a good thing," she mumbled.

"Trust me. Bexley runs a tight ship. You'll have two with you at all times, and our office is locked up tight, no one is getting in."

Her world crashing and all Shelby could think of was falling asleep right here with Jeff to hold her.

"You want to go lay down?"

"I'd rather sit here. If that's okay."

"Fine with me." Jeff propped his feet up on the ottoman and squeezed her shoulders.

AFTER SHELBY FELL ASLEEP a few times on his shoulder, Jeff convinced her to go upstairs and take a nap. Heart pounding, he made his way downstairs and to Buck.

"Problem?" Buck never even looked up.

"What were you discussing with Shelby?"

"The situation surrounding her stay and what it means for the team." Buck looked up, then leaned back in his chair. "I'm assuming you're wanting something more?"

"It just seems odd that you'd want a private conversation about something as non-specific as the reason she's here." Jeff frowned as Buck kept his stare. "You know something more?"

"I know there're other things at play. But that's her place to tell you. Not mine."

Jaw clenching, Jeff paced a moment. "Do you know where Dale Fletcher is?"

"My guys lost him."

"He could be behind this. Finishing what he started."

"No way. Been out of town for most of it."

Jeff sighed. "I finally figured out what's going on with Fredricks. He said there's an interview online of you discussing Dani's kidnapping and the involvement of a police officer."

"What interview?"

"It's online. It didn't take me long to find it. I thought you were clear about speaking to the press about what happened."

Buck stood, his face turning crimson. "The only person I discussed the situation with was the commissioner because he asked to be the one to take my statement. If it was recorded, then he leaked it."

"You'll never be able to prove that, Buck."

Buck shook his head and stepped out from around the desk.

"You can't go after him either."

"I believe I'm the man in charge here, not you," Buck gritted out.

"Yes, you're in charge. But I'm the man giving you a reality check. You've already made him mad, you're on the verge of going to jail if you show up at his home or office. With what they have on your computer, it'd be hard to refute."

Buck stood in place, staring at the door.

"I know you're more than upset about a former friend doing this to you. But we have no play here, not right now. If we lose you, the entire program tanks. You know that."

"What's going on?"

Jeff turned at the sound of Dani's voice. She leaned against the doorway, eyes darting between them.

"Is there another issue?"

"Probably."

Buck shot him a glare.

"That reporter?"

"That's being handled," Buck answered.

"By whom?"

His glare landed on Jeff once more.

"Okay, so if that's being handled, then what else is it?" Dani walked in and took hold of Buck's arm. "I'm getting worried about you. This is all repeating over and over, and I feel like it's my fault."

"It's not you." Buck wrapped her in a hug. "It has nothing to do with you. This is personal, and I think it's about me."

"You know that's not true either. The attacks started small and were never focused on you. It's the whole team."

"Okay, then who benefits if our team goes under?" Dani stepped away from Buck, tears glistening in her eyes.

"The bad guys."

Buck snapped his head to Jeff. "What?"

"The bad guys benefit. The police and the SWAT teams are spread too thin, the response times get longer and the criminals get away with more."

Buck's jaw worked back and forth a moment. "I need a minute," he mumbled as he left the room.

"So, tell me about Shelby."

Jeff turned his attention to Danica. "What about her?"

"Have you decided what you're going to do?"

"About what? The fact she doesn't trust me enough to tell me what's going on?"

Danica rolled her eyes. "Jeff, you've got to give her a break. She's been through so much the past week and needs someone to support her, not give her the third degree."

Jeff shifted from one leg to another. "I get that. But if what she's hiding is what's going on—"

"I thought you said she had no idea who was behind all this?"

"I did—I mean, I believe she has no idea. But the detective mentioned someone, and I wonder if whoever he is could be the reason this is all happening."

Danica sighed and took hold of his arm. "Jeff, if the detective knew who was doing all this, he'd be arresting him, not asking Shelby about him." She patted his arm. "So, you can either step up and be the friend she needs right now, or you can back off and let her deal with this on her own."

"What if—"

"No, no what ifs. You're either in or out. This is the time to decide what you want."

As Danica left, Jeff could feel his whole body heating at the comment. He'd made several comments to both Evan and Haiden throughout the past year about their situations with the women now in their life.

It was so easy to see what was happening from the outside and he had never understood why they didn't get it. Now he did. Fear.

Having a few wonderful kisses last night wasn't a promise or even a gauge to determine if she was anywhere close to where he was at the moment. It was a great response to a stressful situation and he sure wouldn't turn down another response like that. But it was definitely leading him down a road where he could get ripped apart if she didn't feel the same way.

Telling her how he felt and not receiving the same response was terrifying. He'd already lost his heart to this woman and she had no idea. Maybe if she knew, she could find a way to open up to him as well.

Or even worse, he'd fall into the same situation he had with Meline.

That can't happen again, Lord. Please don't let me mess this all up like I did with her.

33

J eff eased up the staircase to find Shelby sitting on the couch, facing the window.

It was now or never.

"Hey, Shelby."

Shelby's head snapped around, her eyes wide. "Oh, hey. I was trying to read. Dani said I could borrow some books." She waved the closed book in her hand.

With a grin, he sat down on the ottoman in front of her. "I wanted to tell you something."

"Jeff, I don't think—"

"Just give me a second. It's important." He leaned forward on his knees, taking a deep breath. "I've watched things collapse with my friends and their relationships. I've seen them fall out over the fact they can't get their own heads wrapped around what it is they want."

Sitting up, she gripped his arm. "I'm not sure this is the best time," she whispered.

"Whatever's going on here, the open doors and bugs, the attack, it's not going to change anything. I care about you, Shelby."

Her wide eyes fluttered.

"Almost ten years ago, I met a woman. Her name was Meline. We started dating, and everything moved so fast, we were engaged and married within six months." He let out a chuckle. "It's definitely not typical for me. I tend to overanalyze."

She offered a smirk.

"Things were great, I finished up training and was getting more and more work in the field. I had just accepted a job with Homeland." Swallowing the urge to change his mind, he let out a breath. "Meline was what you would call a free spirit, another atypical aspect of our relationship. I'd never met anyone like her. As I worked longer hours, she started to feel left out.

"Almost a year later, we both realized we wanted different things. I talked about a family, she wanted to travel with me. It was a constant conversation, and I never could understand why she didn't want what I wanted. She would leave for a few weeks at a time, visiting friends and family all over the county while I worked. It wasn't an answer."

Shelby rested her hand on his. Gripping her fingers, he smiled.

"We spoke every day, and I did my best to get her to change. I was convinced I could make her see my way of things." He shook his head. "I told her she could either come back and share the life I had imagined, or she could make another decision."

"Was that the only way?"

He glanced up at her glassy eyes.

"Was there no other way to share a life together? That she had to give up what she wanted?"

"I was wrong. It was all me, and I was so wrong."

"What did she choose?"

He squeezed her hand before letting it go. "She was in a car accident just outside of the city. She was hit head-on and passed away."

"Jeff. I'm so sorry."

"I am too. I took away her choice, made the decision for her."

"It's not your fault she had an accident."

He shrugged. "No, but I'm certain my ultimatum was the only thing on her mind. She never would've been on that road if I hadn't made the choice for her."

"You can't think that way."

Letting out a deep breath, he forced the words from his mouth. "I've not pushed to date, to find a relationship. God put you in my path for a reason, and I'm not going to wait until things are bad, until it all blows up, to decide I want something more. I'm also not going to make the decision for you."

Her mouth dropped a bit, but nothing came out.

"You don't have to say anything right now, Shelby. But I'd like you to consider trusting me, letting me be here for you in all things, not just this."

Giving her hand a squeeze, he stood and marched down the stairs, hurrying to his room before he did something else stupid.

Leaning against his closed door, the weight of it all lifted. The one thing he'd kept hidden away, now out and shining for Shelby to see, why wasn't it crushing him? The guilt, the pain, the need to control, it always pushed into his chest and took his breath.

But now, for the first time in years, the fact someone else knew and didn't see that side to him, maybe he'd changed that much?

Jesus, please continue to make me more like You. Give me comfort in that.

34

Shelby stared as Jeff left, descending the steps, the echo of his door slamming broke the silence.

Knowing he had some things in his past and hearing that story, it was heartbreaking. However, it did explain why such an amazing guy, a handsome, caring, and God-fearing man was still single.

With a deep breath, she leaned on her knees, her stomach churning. As much as she wanted to tell him, get it all out in the open, it wasn't the right time. Someone like Jeff, working in the chaos and in protection mode all the time, could easily change his mind after all this was over. As heartfelt as his comments came through, she was the worst judge of character when it came to sincerity.

She stood with a grunt, pain radiating down her back. The staples bruised and burned, but it was her heart that ached. Jeff had protected and saved her, offered her so much, it was selfish to hold back. But once he found out, chances were he'd realize just how pathetic she was.

Staring at the stairwell, she shook her head and went to the bedroom, a lump swelling in her throat. After losing so much, if she lost Jeff too because of her bad judgment, it would destroy her too.

"I can't go through this again," she mumbled.

Heart pounding, she grabbed some clothes and headed to the bathroom to change. Jeff's need to keep his wife close wasn't a failure on his part; he hadn't forced her hand, no matter what he believed.

But allowing Ryan in, letting him get away with everything right under her nose and deceiving her to the extent of committing crimes in her name, was on her. Wiping away tears, she stared at her haggard face in the mirror.

Lord, give me something to cling to besides Jeff. He deserves so much better.

"I HAVE to go to the station?" Shelby looked across the kitchen island at Jeff, her face heating.

After a restless night's sleep, Shelby had awoken to Jeff knocking on her door. Dressing and then meeting him in the kitchen came with the news of a meeting at the police station.

"Detective Fredricks wants to speak with you." He sat down a mug of coffee in front of her.

"But can't he come here?"

Jeff walked around and sat next to her. "We'll be there too. Don't worry."

Worry was all she had now. No sleep last night, no peace; her mind rushed through with all the things she needed to tell Jeff, her past, her fears.

"Something on your mind?"

Letting out a sigh, she focused on the coffee. It was about all she had to cling to at the moment.

"Shelby?"

"I'm just tired."

"I'm sorry you're not sleeping. I promise, all this will get cleared up, and you'll be able to get some real sleep before you start your job back at the clinic."

She grunted and sat down her mug. "Are you always a glass-half-full person and perky in the morning?"

He chuckled and leaned against her shoulder. "Comes with the job. Early hours, lots of coffee and it does help to get to see you too."

Her jaw dropped as he stood to go back to the stove.

"So, how do you like your eggs?"

"Uh, scrambled is fine."

"Over easy and two of them." Evan walked into the room, a grin on his face. "Since you're cooking and all."

Jeff shot him a glare and then went to work at the stove.

She took a sip of her coffee. "So, when's the big day?"

Evan's smile grew bigger. "We've got three weeks left."

"Nervous?"

"Hah." Jeff offered from the stove.

"Of course he's not nervous." Bexley appeared from the stairwell, her bright red curls bouncing in a ponytail. "But we are anxious." She patted Evan's chest.

"How're you guys going to work together and be married?" Shelby leaned in as Jeff chuckled. "What? What's so funny?"

Jeff turned around. "I'm not sure they've thought that far ahead."

"We have." Bexley hung her hands on her hips as she glared at Jeff. "But unlike you, we have a healthy working relationship with everyone. Buck's already working on a schedule to keep us both on or off, and then once Haiden and Danica get married—"

"Wait." Shelby smiled. "So you are all coupled up except for Jeff?"

"And Buck," Evan added.

"Jeff likes to think of himself as the lone wolf." Bexley motioned with her fingers.

Shelby chuckled and tried to hide her amusement behind her mug as Jeff turned around with a plateful of eggs.

"I hear you laughing, and yes, it has fit me for a long time." He gave her a wink and turned back to the stove.

"He also thinks he's the giver of knowledge, handing out free advice." Bexley patted him on the back as she walked past.

"And does the advice work?"

"Well, let's see." Jeff turned with another plate of over-easy eggs. "Bexley and Evan are getting hitched, and Danica and Haiden are eloping at some point, so I'd say I'm four for four on the advice."

"Eloping? Seriously?"

Jeff's face went red as Bexley stared. "Um, yeah, maybe? Did she not tell you they were thinking about that?"

"No, she never mentioned it."

"Good job, lone wolf," Evan mumbled as he took his plate and sat down at the other end of the kitchen island.

"Well, I mean, can you really see Haiden and Dani in front of a lot of people? All that attention on them?"

"I don't know. I guess I wasn't really thinking about it."

"Maybe we should elope." Evan grinned as Bexley gave him a glare.

"Not funny, Evan."

Shelby grimaced. "I think I'll take my plate into the living room." Picking her plate up, she balanced it and the coffee as she walked to the couch.

"Your stitches are bleeding."

She paused as Jeff took her cup. "I wanted it to air out last night so I didn't cover it with gauze. All the tossing and turning, I guess I made it bleed."

Jeff took the plate too. "Go change. I'll keep this warm." His bright blue eyes stared her down, pushing all those feelings back up she'd been working to keep bottled.

It would be all too easy to just lean in ...

"Shelby?"

Coming back to reality, she let out a breath. "Thanks."

Easing up the staircase, she stepped into the room with a huff.

"Everything okay?"

She leaned her head back against the door. "Great. Perfect."

Danica let out a chuckle. "So, what's going on down there?"

"I feel I should warn you. Jeff let out a comment about you eloping, and Bexley seemed ... surprised."

Danica groaned and fell back in her bed. "Great, just great."

"Was it a secret?"

"No." Danica sat up as Shelby took a seat at the desk. "But I was trying to keep from bringing everything up right now. She and Evan are getting married soon, and I want this to be about them, not about Haiden and me."

"You're a good friend, Dani."

"Well, I obviously have some work to do." She stood from the bed. "You coming?"

"Oh, can you put some gauze on my back? I think my stitches keep bleeding." Shelby dug through her bag and produced a new shirt and a gauze wrap.

"You always carry emergency supplies with you wherever you go?"

Shelby chuckled. "Actually, much more than I should probably admit. But especially with this cut, I've been trying to keep it taken care of so it doesn't scar so bad."

"It looks pretty good." Dani finished wrapping the gauze and taped it. "You're good to go. Just soak that shirt in the sink so it doesn't stain."

"Thanks."

"Hey."

She turned with a sigh, Dani's dark hair falling into her face as she tilted her head.

"It's going to be good. I'm sure the police will figure out who's doing this, and then you can go back to normal life."

"I know, it's just unnerving. All this, all at once ... I can't take a breath."

"I think this is more than just the attacks."

Shelby frowned at Dani's grin. "It's about all of it. Jeff mentioned someone and what happened and I just—"

"Meline? He told you about her?"

Shelby nodded as Danica sat down, her jaw hanging open.

"Wow. That's big. He never talks about her."

"I guess you were there."

"Yeah, it was ... crazy. Jeff's a straight arrow in everything, and Meline was his opposite. When she passed, Jeff just kept saying it was his fault."

"That's what he said to me. How can he think that? He's got all this education in reading people and understanding how people think. How could he hold on to all that?"

Danica sighed. "He's lost a lot in his life but he's always shrugged it off as if it were nothing. His faith has pulled him through, but I think he feels it was his decision to make. Even though I don't think that's what happened."

"What do you mean?"

"Jeff wanted a certain lifestyle and family, and he always told me she didn't want that. But it was her choice to come back, which is what she was doing. I think she wanted it much more than what he believed."

Shelby nodded.

"Look, Jeff's like a brother to me. He's always there for me and I know he doesn't just take a risk for anyone. He's a good guy that would protect whoever needs it, but take a risk, I'm not so sure. Just so you know, he's taking a risk on you."

Shelby's face heated. "I—"

"Just wait." Danica stood. "I know you're living in a chaos-filled world right now. When that dies down, you'll have a decision to make. Whatever you choose will be the right choice for you and for Jeff. I think you have a much better idea of who he is than anyone else."

"Even you?"

Danica laughed. "Yes, definitely me. We've always been close, but when it comes to relationships, we've had this line in the sand. So yes, I think you're the best person to see what's on his mind and in his heart." Danica turned and headed for the door. "See you down there."

Shelby sat watching the empty room for a moment. Jeff had laid out his heart, and she did see it all too clearly. But there was one thing that would shatter that clarity, and talking about it all seemed impossible.

"God, give me the right time and place," she mumbled as she pushed herself to stand and headed for the bathroom, shirt in hand.

35

"Thanks for coming down."

Jeff walked Shelby into the conference room with Detective Fredricks.

"I've been on the phone with the Tampa police."

"Why?" Jeff leaned against the table as Shelby shrunk down in the chair.

Fredricks cut his eyes between Jeff and Shelby. "Well, it appears we have some answers."

"Great. You know who's doing all this?"

"I've got a good idea. I've spoken to several officers in Tampa, and Officer Duncan's name came up several times."

Jeff's jaw clenched. Obviously, there was someone else at play, and he wasn't privy to any of the information surrounding the situation. "Who's Officer Duncan?"

"He's the parole officer for Ryan Cushing."

Jeff paused, waiting for the punch.

"It seems they've brought up charges against him for parolee violations."

Jeff heard the slight gasp from Shelby. "And that means?"

"It means he's being paid to falsify documents. He's taking bribes to let parolees jump ship."

"What?" Shelby's voice cracked as her body stiffened. "But you just told me, you said the other day—"

"I just learned all this, Dr. Durning. Ryan Cushing isn't the only case that's been compromised. Duncan's got five other released parolees he was supposed to be keeping tabs on that have left town. One was arrested last night, and they started digging. That's how the Tampa police found out about the others."

"Where's Duncan now?" Jeff gritted out.

Fredricks shrugged. "No idea. We've put out an all-points bulletin and have eyes looking for him. But now, I'm much more concerned about what this means for you. You testified against him, correct?"

Testified?

She nodded, feverishly wiping the tears from her cheeks. "I ... I was part of it."

Jeff's face heated as he tried to put the pieces together. "Part of what?"

Her red eyes glanced up. "When things weren't adding up at work, and the pharmacy started calling, I went straight to the police with my lawyer. We told them everything, and they wanted to be able to round up the entire group, not just Ryan."

"Ryan Cushing? The guy you mentioned yesterday?" Jeff stood as Fredricks nodded. "So you not only testified against this Ryan guy, you were involved in his capture?"

"Yes."

"What was it? What was he doing?"

Shelby pulled at the jacket sleeves. "He'd been stealing my prescription pads, selling them, and forging my name. It almost destroyed my entire career," she whispered.

"He's here for revenge."

"What? Revenge? I have nothing left." She stood, glaring at Fredricks. "He took my life from me. It took me years to find another job. I moved from Florida to get away from all of that."

"Whether you want to believe it or not, this is all coming

together because of him. Now that we know who's behind all this, we know who to look for. I suggest you keep yourself safe."

"Not an issue," Jeff said as Fredricks left. He motioned to the door and walked out, Shelby in tow.

"Jeff. Please."

Jeff let out a deep breath. "Why didn't you just tell me?"

"I tried, I did. But it's so humiliating, and the detective assured me that Ryan was still in Florida and ..." she wiped her face and leaned against the wall. "I didn't think you'd understand."

"No, I don't." He paused in front of her. "Explain it to me."

Shaking her head, her cheeks turned crimson. "I lost everyone," she whispered. "When this all came out, I lost friends, colleagues, even my family was embarrassed to be around me."

"And you didn't trust me? What does it take, Shelby? What does it take to earn your trust? Because after all we've been through, I don't know what else I can do."

Her body shook as she rushed down the hallway toward the parking lot. "Shelby!" Jeff took chase, sprinting out the side doors.

"Stop!"

Jeff stepped outside to see an SUV pulling up to the sidewalk and a man shoving Shelby into the back seat. "No!" He took off after the SUV, but it was too late. He watched helplessly as they pulled away. Sprinting down the road, he pulled out his phone. "Evan!"

"What's going on?"

"They took her."

"I'm outside, there's no one else here."

"The side alley." Turning the corner, the SUV was gone. "Swing around to the back and follow the road to the north side of the building. I'm about a block over. I'm calling Fredricks." Hanging up he dialed the detective.

"Powers?"

"Shelby was just kidnapped. Dark SUV, tags distorted, I need the footage."

"What? Outside our building?"

Screeching tires echoed behind him. Barely jumping out of the way, he landed on his side as the dark sedan sideswiped him. Men filed out of the car, converging. Gun out, Jeff couldn't get it aimed before two men grabbed his arms.

Landing a punch to one, he managed to get the man down before collapsing at a hit to the stomach. Blocking another punch, he kicked out and was yanked down from behind. A hit to the face and spots filled his vision.

"Get him inside. Now!"

36

Louis leaned back in his chair, a cigar in his mouth and the phone to his ear.

"I can't do anything else. You made the wrong move."

Louis huffed. "I did your job for you."

"You can't bring judgment on someone that's not done anything wrong, not in my position. Attempting to take down Thompson like that, I tried to warn you that he's got friends in high places."

"Either way, I'm done playing nice. I asked Carver to take care of things the right way, and he danced around a direct hit. From now on, only direct hits."

"I won't take out anyone for this."

"Then you'll lose your life."

"I've done a lot of bad things in my lifetime. But I'm not a killer. I won't be involved. I don't know how you got that information on Buck, but it's a career-ender. That reporter, she'll give you up."

The call ended and Louis set the phone on the desk. For a man in such a high position, he was weak. And a weak man could be bent. It was becoming clearer and clearer, another loose end

215

to handle had presented itself and he was now without help to take care of it.

Staring out the window, he knew he needed more people in the right place if he were to stay in power. People he could control. The reporter failed and wouldn't be an issue. Nothing could possibly be traced back to him. Carver, perhaps, but not him.

It still didn't take care of the one group he needed removed. But the lynchpin was the key.

The phone beeped.

Meeting tonight for my payment. Once I'm done with him, I expect results from you.

You will. Once I win. I will need your help with another loose end, one that no one seems to be able to handle.

Who?

Buck Thompson

JEFF SQUINTED as the blindfold was removed. "It's not like you had to blindfold me."

A punch to the face and he let out a grunt as his mouth filled with blood. Pain surged through his jaw, shooting through his head.

"I think you better keep your mouth shut."

The large man in front of him glared down, rubbing his fist. The face familiar, Jeff worked his jaw, giving him time to see the red-head from the video.

"If it isn't Bruce. Can't believe you're acting as if your fist hurts so badly. You've got terrible form."

The man punched again, throwing Jeff's head to the other

side. Allowing his head to hang, he spit up the blood pooling in his mouth.

"Keep it up, funny man."

Straightening, Jeff decided he could wait a bit to push the punisher's buttons.

"So, you're the guy." A man walked through the doorway, a grin on his face. "I was hoping you'd be a cop. We could use another cop."

"A cop for what?"

Jeff closed his eyes as Bruce's fist made contact once more. Shooting pain burned through his jaw.

"We've got a need for some insider information." The guy obviously in charge took a seat next to him.

"Where's Shelby?" Jeff managed to get out.

"We're just letting her stew a bit. She's more manageable if she's all worked up and worried."

Jeff glared at the man's smile.

"Trust me, I know what I'm doing." The man winked.

"Who're you?" Jeff mumbled.

"Someone that needs an answer." The boss leaned in. "Either you're with us or not."

"Not."

Another hit and Jeff coughed up some more blood, his jaw aching.

"We can do this all day. As far as inside guys, it's not like you're the only one. But we need a boots-on-the-street kind of man, someone in the middle of the chaos and can ever so slightly direct it away."

"Wrong man," he muttered, bracing as another hit to stomach had him gasp for air, spots filling his vision once more.

"You see, I've been watching you and your team. You're not all that proficient at keeping a low profile. I know about all of you, and I know about your little relationship with Shelby." The man frowned. "It seems my predecessor wasn't getting anywhere pushing you guys out of the way. But I'll handle that myself."

"Out of the way of what?"

"You're in the zone, the one place that my new friends need to be. The TRT disrupts that area, keeps interfering with my friend's work when you respond so quickly. It's not suitable for business."

"You work for the Russians?"

The man grinned. "I'm what you call a self-made man. I work for myself. Whatever angle pays the best. Right now, you're in the way of all of that."

"So the Russians want you to get rid of the team. Are you behind all the attacks?"

"Nope, that was before my time. I take a more direct course of action." The man glared. "The question is, are you willing to play along, or will we need to move you out of the way along with the rest of the team?"

"I might consider it if you let Shelby go."

Another hit, and Jeff did his best to stay conscious.

"Wrong answer. But since you're so keen on what's going on with Shelby, why don't you come along with me?"

Letting out a groan at the pain radiating from his shoulders, Jeff stood as directed, shoved and prodded down the hallway. The only way he could think to get himself out of this was agreeing to the man's terms. Although, he figured the terms wouldn't hold up for long.

God, show me what I need to do to get us out safe.

Turning into the room, the door flew open and Shelby sat tied to a chair, with a tearstained face and her arms bound.

"Jeff!"

37

"Jeff?"

"I'm good." Jeff forced a smile as he finally got out an answer. They shoved him into a chair and he stiffened at the pain.

"I'm so sorry," Shelby murmured as tears soaked her cheeks.

"So, are you going to introduce us?"

Jeff glared up at the boss, another grin on his face.

"Why're you doing this?"

"Oh, come now. I think you know why. I've been sitting around just thinking about how easy you got off." The man sat down in front of her. "It's been a long three years."

Jeff's jaw clenched. This must be Ryan. The stakes just went up.

"It was all you. I didn't do anything, you manipulated and destroyed my life," she shouted as her face turned red.

"And now, you'll pay for turning me in. For destroying *my* life."

"I'm not going through this again."

"Yes, I think you are." Ryan stood, pulling a gun and aiming it at Jeff's head.

"No!" Shelby screamed, attempting to stand with her hands bound behind her back.

"He won't work for us, so that leaves a loose end. My new friends don't like loose ends, and I'm not about to disappoint them again."

"Stop! I'll do whatever you want. But you have to leave him alone."

Ryan leaned in, glaring down at Shelby. He slowly turned to Jeff. "By the way, we've not been introduced. I'm Ryan, Shelby's ex-fiancé." A phone buzzed and Ryan answered, turning toward the door.

Ex-fiancé? It all made sense. Jeff did what he could to get Shelby's attention. "Hey, we're okay."

She shook her head, her body leaned over as her arms straightened from behind.

"Lean back, it'll ease your arms."

"So, you ready?"

Jeff glared up at Ryan. "Ready for what?"

"Not you, her."

"Leave her out of it."

A hit to the face and Jeff was straining to take in a breath as pain surged.

"Leave him alone!"

"Why? Why is he so important? You did what you could to get me arrested and we were about to be married."

"I didn't know who you were," she gritted. "Besides, what does it matter to you? I'll make you a deal. You like deals if I remember correctly."

Ryan huffed.

"I'll go with you, do whatever it is you need me to do and you leave him alone. If not, I'll become very difficult to deal with. And I think you can understand that," she hissed.

"Just what do you think you can do? I can take him apart, piece by piece."

This time Shelby let out a scoff. "You're barely hanging on as it is. Blood isn't your thing, remember?"

Ryan's face paled as he cut his eyes between Shelby and Jeff. "Fine. You try to escape, you try anything, I call Bruce here to take care of your new ... friend."

Ryan pulled out a knife and released Shelby's hands and ankles. She rushed over to Jeff, grabbing on to his neck.

"I'll handle this, okay? I'll take care of all of it," she whispered into his ear.

"Don't worry about me. I'll be fine." Searching her eyes, Jeff hated the fact she'd blame herself. "Whatever happens, I'm sorry I didn't trust you. This isn't on you."

"Let's go." Ryan yanked her away, her yelp echoing in the room. As the door slammed, Jeff measured up Bruce once more.

"You know that's all a lie, right?"

"It is what it is. You want to tell me what's the big deal about Shelby being in the middle of all whatever this is? I thought he wanted revenge."

"All that other stuff was just to get back at her, he scared her pretty good. But we can't get into a safe without the code." Bruce chuckled. "I guess we could, but I'm not bringing down a whole building when the doc can just open it. Ryan's good at pushing her buttons."

Jeff took a haggard breath as Bruce produced a knife. "Setting me free, huh?"

"Looks like you've not been worn down enough if you've still got a sense of humor."

As Bruce pushed into his space, Jeff headbutted the man and sprang to his feet. Turning, he slammed Bruce to the ground with the chair, administering a swift kick to keep the man down. Bruce lay there, panting but unconscious.

On his knees, he rotated until his hand was able to reach the knife now on the floor. Sawing through the ropes, he freed one hand, then easily freed the other.

A search of Bruce produced a phone.

"Who's this?" Buck's ragged voice sounded.

"It's me."

"Where're you?"

"No idea," Jeff mumbled. "Ryan just took Shelby. I think they're going to her office? Wherever there's a safe and something worth stealing."

"What?"

"Look, I'm in a room, and I'm fairly certain I'm not the only one here." He snatched the knife back up.

"I'm tracing the call, keep the phone on."

Jeff lowered the phone to the floor as scuffling sounds came from the other side of the door.

"Bruce?"

Angling the knife in his hand, Jeff ignored the pounding in his head and the pain pulsing through his jaw as he pushed into the wall behind the door.

The door clicked and opened.

"Bruce?"

Grabbing the man's arm, Jeff spun him around and slammed him into the wall, holding the knife to his throat.

"Are there any more?"

The man's wide eyes held fear as he shook his head. "No, no, everyone else left."

"Where'd they go?"

"I ... I don't know. I'm not in that part of the meet. I don't know."

Turning the man to the wall, Jeff pulled the man's arm up high behind his back.

"Then we wait." Breathing heavy, Jeff rested his hand on the man's shoulder, the blade against his back.

"Jeff? Jeff if you can hear me, the police should be there soon!" Buck's voice echoed through the cell phone.

"Go find Shelby! Check her office building!"

"Copy!"

Sirens echoed in the distance, and Jeff sighed in relief.

God, protect her. Save her.

38

S itting in the back of an SUV, Shelby tried to pray, but the words wouldn't come.

Having Ryan back in her life sent shockwaves through her body; anger and fear that he had been released and no one told her, no one gave her warning. And now Jeff was in danger as well.

"Something on your mind?"

She glared at Ryan. "How did you even get out? Your minimum sentence was ten years. It's been three."

"Four, one year served." He winked. "My lawyer's very good. With the over-population issues and the fact I'm not a hardened criminal with no personal injury charges, I was set free."

"Why find me?" That was the question that needed answering. "I'm not in Florida anymore, and there's no reason for you to follow me here."

"First, I have a contact here. If you remember, I took a lot of trips to Dallas."

She eased her fingers over the cuts on her wrist. "I've chosen to forget that entire portion of my life. I don't remember any of it," she hissed.

"Of course you remember. But when I found out you were here too, it all came together."

223

"You tried to kill me, Ryan. You filled my house with gas and then tried to run me over! Now what?"

Ryan chuckled and leaned back in the seat. "You'll see. It'll be like old times."

The comment hung in the air, sucking the life from her body. What did that mean? What could he possibly want with her now? And what about Jeff?

Her heart burst as tears streamed down her cheeks once more. In her haste to keep her secrets, she'd put Jeff in harm's way. The entire thing was her fault. As inept as she was with relationships, she was obviously worse as a friend.

"We're here." A hushed voice from the front echoed in the quiet vehicle.

"Hang out in back. They should arrive soon."

"Who?"

Ryan ignored her.

Looking out the window, she realized they were at her office. Vomit rose in her throat. He'd been following her, knew about the clinic and all the drugs the doctors had access to through the on-site pharmacy.

"Did you send Terry Quarters after me? To kill me?"

"That was a buddy of mine's idea. It was just for a little revenge, then you had to go and get him killed." Ryan glared. "It all turned out for the best. I made it here earlier than anticipated and was able to pick up where Dierks left off. The bugs, the doors, I wanted you to feel just as out of control as I did sitting there watching you testify against me.

"You have no idea what I'm capable of, Shelby. But I think you're getting there. As for Terry, he was a loose end I was asked to take care of. He was supposed to bring you to me, but once again, he failed."

Swallowing the bile, she closed her eyes.

Lord, please stop them from hurting more people. Send whoever can be of help, whoever can make them stop. Be with Jeff and give him protection.

"We're in the big time now." He leaned in, dark eyes glaring right through her. "You better do what I say. These guys aren't like the others—they'll kill you where you stand. If you play your cards right, you'll make it out of this alive."

He yanked her arm and she muffled a yelp as she landed on the pavement. Gripping her wrist, bloodied from being bound, she stared at the SUV parked next to the one she had just exited.

A large man opened the door and a dark-haired man in a suit stepped onto the sidewalk.

"Hey, Miikka. I told you I could deliver." Ryan grinned and offered a handshake, which Miikka declined.

Miikka's eyes leveled on her. Her whole body shivered as her heart raced. The man was evil, she could see it in his cold eyes.

"Let's get this straight, Cushing. The only reason you're not dead is our mutual friend said you were good. I expect results." The accent-laced words hung in the air. It wasn't just her life on the line.

"No worries." Ryan's voice went up a notch.

She was prodded in the back and forced up to the door. Her badge appeared.

"Let's get inside."

Glaring at Ryan, she snatched the badge. Maybe the cameras and the crew monitoring the clinic would see what was happening and send help.

Swiping the badge, she put in her code. The door popped open and Ryan shoved her inside.

If only the help would get there in time.

"Oh my goodness." Danica covered her mouth.

Jeff slid from the taxi and ignored Danica's commentary and the look on her face as he approached a frowning Buck.

"You should be in a hospital."

"Where is she? You have a visual?"

"Haiden, you good?"

"Got her," the muffled response came through the radio.

Buck nodded, staring up at Jeff. "Let's get focused. SWAT should be here soon and we've got to find a way to advance without those men out front seeing us coming."

Fredricks walked up, grimacing as he looked Jeff up and down.

"Thanks for getting in touch with Buck." Jeff nodded.

"I knew you would want him involved. I'm sorry it's all going down like this. If we'd known sooner about Cushing, we might've been able to divert all this."

"It's not your fault. It's ours. She was under our protection."

Bexley and Danica flanked him. "You need to sit down."

"I'm fine," Jeff mumbled through a swollen lip as he stared at the building ahead of them.

"You look bad." Evan appeared, cell phone in hand as he stared at Jeff a moment, then handed off the phone to Buck. "FBI's been calling. Apparently, once Fredricks started poking around about Ryan's probable contacts in the area, the FBI took notice." He motioned to Fredricks. "They tried calling you and can't get through, so they called us. They want point. Something about an ongoing investigation."

"Good with me. We need all the help we can get." Buck took the phone. "Buck Thompson. What ongoing investigation?"

Jeff edged closer, pulling down the phone so he could hear.

"That's classified, sir."

"Well, un-classify it. We've got a civilian hostage in the middle, and one of my guys has been abducted and put through the wringer. I need answers."

"This is Special Agent Nathan Peters. Who's this?"

"Buck Thompson, head of the TRT and the reason you're about to get the drug dealer you've apparently been looking for. I want answers."

"You'll get them. But not over the phone. We're on our way, let's get this taken care of first."

"Fine with me."

The call ended and Buck turned back to Jeff. "You need to sit this one out. It's not going to be an easy one, and she'll need you when we're done."

Jeff blew out a deep breath. "Fine."

"We'll get her, Jeff."

Jeff glanced at Danica. "She thinks it's all her fault. I couldn't tell her ... I need to tell her," he whispered.

"Then wait here. We'll bring her to you."

SUVs flooded the area and Buck turned to Fredricks.

"Did you talk to the FBI about all this?"

Fredricks shook his head. "Cushing has a lot of contacts here, one being Dierks Carver."

Jeff walked closer. "Carver? Seriously? You didn't make the connection sooner?"

"Sorry, we didn't look at Cushing too hard once we were told he was still in Tampa. It seemed more like a local issue with a patient. We were working that angle when I heard from Tampa police this morning."

"Are you Buck Thompson?"

Buck nodded and shook the man's hand. "Agent Peters?"

The man nodded and turned to Fredricks. "You are?"

"Detective Fredricks. You want to tell us what's going on here? Why is a two-bit thief involved with a drug cartel?"

"Not just a drug cartel. The guy's name is Mikhail Ivanov or Miikka. Bad guy with a bad rap. But that's not the worst part."

"What's the worst part?" Buck asked.

"Cushing and Miika have bad blood. The file on Miika shows he's been working on moving into the area for the past six years with no luck. He's made a lot of enemies and has pushed a lot of buttons. Cushing was suspected to be involved in several of Ivanov's operations."

"He worked for Ivanov?" Fredricks questioned.

"Ryan mentioned being a self-made man. He works for

whoever pays him," Jeff mumbled, rubbing his jaw and attempting to ignore the pain sweeping through his body.

"Yeah, he got paid, but Ivanov didn't. Guy skipped town owing big. Ivanov had a price on his head. Pulled it the other day."

"So Ryan's walking into a bad situation with bad blood." Jeff's heart pounded. She was in more danger than she could possibly know.

Peters nodded. "You got eyes?"

"Sniper in that building." Buck pointed out where Haiden was waiting. "He's on point."

Peters motioned as men in FBI gear came forward. "My guys will join. Just as soon as we get set up, we'll take out the men in the front, then follow upwards."

"If these guys are cartel, they won't be easy."

Peters frowned at him. "I take it you're the one they had?"

Jeff nodded.

"Look, we've done our research on this group. Two at the door, two at the elevator, and probably two with Ivanov at the top. He travels heavy."

"They'll be at least one more with Ryan in the middle. He left with a few men and Shelby."

"But why go after Shelby?" Danica stood staring between them.

"Payment," Jeff answered, finally seeing the full picture of what Bruce had mentioned. "Ryan came here for revenge on Shelby for setting him up. He's been following her, he knows where she works. The hospital isn't someplace he can hit, but there's a safe in the clinic, one that only a doctor can open. They're going for the drugs. Which I'm guessing is the payment he owes to Ivanov."

"Then, what happens to Shelby when they get them?" Bexley whispered, staring from Jeff to Evan.

"My guys are ready. Let's go." Peters motioned and headed toward the building.

"We'll get her. You know we will." Danica squeezed Jeff's arm before they ran from the lot and converged on the building.

Swallowing the burning lump in his throat, Jeff leaned against the SUV to keep from falling over.

"Lord, protect the team, protect Shelby. Bring her back to me," he whispered as shouts echoed and teams converged on the building.

39

On the elevator, Shelby couldn't help the trembling of her body. Ryan wrapped an arm around her shoulders, but in the small box, she couldn't move away.

"Take it easy, Shelby," he hissed. Stepping from the elevator, his hand pushed her down the hallway. "Here. Get us in."

"Do you have my keys?"

"It's a number lock," he muttered, those piercing eyes set on her. "Open it."

Using the offered badge, she swiped and punched in the number.

"Good girl."

Gritting her teeth at his comment, she stepped inside.

"All the cabinets are locked. We need them opened, now. And the safe. I know you've got a code for that too."

She turned to rebut when a slap slammed her to the wall.

Ryan glared, fuming as his face turned red. "Now!"

Straightening, she backed into the room, her cheek on fire. With trembling hands, she swiped her badge and put in the code for the lock box of keys and began to open the cabinets.

"See? Told you she was gold. This'll be the easiest bust you'll ever—"

A gunshot rang out and she screamed as Ryan's body fell into the room. Miikka stepped inside, the smell of gunpowder wafting into the room as he pointed the gun at her.

"Open the rest."

"You'll just ... you'll just kill me," she stuttered through sobs, her eyes focused on the gun.

"Maybe, maybe not. I'm giving you an option right now. Open the cabinets or die."

Finding the next key, she struggled to get the lock open. "Why ... why did you kill him?"

"He's a nuisance and outlived his usefulness. I told him not to come back to Dallas. He should've listened."

Shaking, she slowly picked her way around the room. "I ... I have to have another set of keys for the safe. It requires two keys," she whispered.

A clang and a silver set of keys appeared on the floor. Bending to pick them up, she entered both sets in the safe and put in her code, then swung the door open. Boxes of high-end pain killers lined the shelves.

"The rest of the cabinets. Now."

The reflection of the downtown buildings shone through the window, and she thought of the last time she was in trouble. Jeff had come in to save her, and Haiden had killed the man holding her hostage with a shot through the window.

"Hurry it up."

As she opened the last cabinet, she pushed herself into the corner, out of the line of the window.

Please, Lord. Please help me.

40

A loud clatter and the blast of gunfire sent Shelby to the ground, covering her head as shouts and glass broke around her.

"Shelby!"

Buck's familiar voice sounded and she reached up, allowing him to pull and prod her through. Stopping at the sight of Ryan's dead body, she heaved to the side, emptying her stomach.

Hearing nothing but the ringing in her ears, she collapsed. Within seconds, her body became weightless as her head pounded.

"Stay with me, Doc."

"Jeff? Is Jeff okay?"

"He's waiting on you."

Buck's voice sounded far away as her eyes closed and darkness took over.

JEFF PACED THE ROOM, barely able to stand. Shelby was unconscious and bruised. Her face was swollen on one side, her wrists raw and bloody from being cuffed. If only he had tried harder.

All at once, her hands fisted and her bleary eyes opened.

"Shelby?"

She blinked a few times as he stepped to the side, leaning against her bed.

"Shelby, you're safe."

"Are you okay?" Her whispered words meant more to him than he could imagine.

"I'm fine." He took her hand and she pulled back, tears already streaming from the corners of her eyes. "Hey, it's fine. We're okay."

"Jeff, I ..." She licked her lips and groaned as the bed rose, allowing her to sit up. "Jeff, we're not okay," she whispered. "I'm so sorry, for all of it, and you can't just ignore—"

He leaned in, and her whole body shifting away from him drove a nail into his chest. "I'm not ignoring anything. I'm here to tell you I'm sorry."

"You didn't do anything wrong."

"Yes, I did. Trying to blame you for not telling me about all this, that wasn't the issue. I was too mad that I couldn't stop it, I couldn't make you feel safe enough."

A shaky hand reached out and he helped her with the cup on the table. After a few sips, she wiped her face.

"I did this," she whispered. "I left you in the dark, and because of that, this happened."

"This happened because a bad guy, lots of bad guys, tried to do something bad. It's not your fault."

The look on her face, he knew exactly what it meant. Shelby was an amazing woman who had his heart, and by that look, she was fixing to break it.

"I ... I can't do this. I almost got you killed." Her lips trembled as she tried to take a breath.

"Shelby, I'm not blaming you—"

"I am." Her pretty amber eyes cut to his. "This is all my fault whether you want to believe it or not. I won't bring you down or put you in the middle of all this. I know what it can do to someone's life. I think you should go."

Attempting to find words to say, he stood there dumbfounded, a lump forming in his throat. "Call me when you're ready."

Resisting every urge to reach out, he left her room, crushed.

Sitting in the waiting area, Jeff held his aching head. He couldn't make himself leave. It was too much to walk away from her after seeing Ryan take her away like that.

"Mr. Powers?"

He straightened. There stood Randal Goodwin.

"Randal? How ... what're you doing here?"

"I was released this morning. Thanks to you." Randal sat down next to him with a frown. "You don't look so good."

"I'm not."

"I heard about the doctor on the news, they said she was in a local hospital and I was hoping I guessed right."

Jeff nodded and leaned back in the chair with a grimace.

"I'm sorry."

He glanced at Randal. "Why?"

"All of this, I should've remembered sooner. Then she would've been safe."

"She should've been safe with me. It's not your fault they took her. It's mine."

"Is she safe now?"

Jeff nodded.

"The DA said she wanted me in counseling for my over-reactions."

"Detective Fredricks defended your situation?" Jeff attempted a smile.

"Yeah. He said after watching the video over and over and the things you said, it was too much to ignore. The family said they'd meet with me tomorrow after the hearing. I wanted to apologize to the little girl. I don't want her to be scared."

"I'm glad he listened."

"If it weren't for you pushing, I'd still be in that cell and would be going away for a long time. Thanks."

Jeff shook Randal's outstretched hand. "Thank you. After what you remembered, we were able to piece it together."

Randal shook his head. "Not soon enough." He stood and paced. "Why don't you go home? I'll stay here."

"Why're you staying? She's safe now."

Randal chuckled. "You need rest. You won't get rest if she's alone. I'll stay and keep watch."

Jeff let out a grunt as he stood. "Thanks."

"You need a ride? I don't think you can see so good."

"I'll make it." He slapped Randal's shoulder as he passed.

As much as he didn't want to leave, she had requested space, and he needed to give it to her. And Randal was right. Just knowing he was here, keeping watch over the place she seemed the least safe in, gave him a sense of peace.

"God, watch over her, please. Let her forgive herself," he whispered as he stepped into the open elevator.

Pulling up in the back alley behind the TRT, Jeff paused as Buck walked up to the SUV from his evening jog.

"Take it things didn't go well?"

Jeff shook his head and turned to the garage to park. "What's that?"

Movement in the darkness shifted around the corner of the building.

Pulling his service weapon, he slid from the SUV.

"No, shine your lights," Buck whispered, weapon raised.

Shifting the SUV into drive, he angled the lights.

"Whoever you are, I'm armed and willing to shoot first and ask questions later. Step out." Buck shouted.

"Don't shoot!" A lanky man stepped from the shadows, arms up and wide eyes. "Just don't shoot. I'm unarmed."

"Who're you?" Buck took several steps forward.

"Dale?" Jeff slid from the SUV, his eyes adjusting to the bright SUV lights in the darkness. "Are you Dale Fletcher?"

"How did you know?"

Buck lowered his weapon. "Because I've been looking for you."

41

Jeff stared at Dale Fletcher sitting in his office with a bottle of water clutched between his trembling hands.

Buck glared down at Dale. "I want to know everything."

"Only if you can offer me protection. I need protection."

"From whom?"

"They're trying to kill me!" Dale's wide eyes stared up at Jeff. "I've been followed ever since I left town."

Buck muffled his chuckle. "Those were my guys."

Dale shook his head and leaned back.

"Give me something I can work with. I need something to take to the police."

"No, no police. That's why I came here. I can't trust the police."

Buck slid the chair from the desk and sat down. "Enlighten me."

"Tell me you'll protect me."

"You give me whatever you've got and I'll keep you safe. You can bet on it. But I do have to make a call."

"No police," Dale hissed.

"Do you know Marty DeSalis?" Buck questioned.

Dale let out a heavy breath. "No."

"Then he's the one to call."

Buck stepped away as Jeff stood staring.

"Tell me you didn't have anything to do with the kidnapping."

"Look, I don't do that kind of stuff. We worked with Adil and he made a phone call. But other than that, we didn't do nothing."

"He's on his way." Buck entered the room.

Jeff nodded. "I want to know the plan. Why us? Why attack us and why risk everything? Who hired you?"

"Give it till Marty gets here. He needs to know too."

Jeff's heart pounded and his body ached. Maybe now they could get answers and close this whole thing up. Then there was Shelby.

Swallowing the lump in this throat, he prayed. *Lord, please help her forgive herself. Give her Your peace, peace that surpasses all understanding. Heal her body and soul.*

BUCK WALKED INTO THE ROOM, Detective Marty DeSalis in tow.

"What? Are you kidding me?" Marty glared, slack-jawed between them.

"Just take a seat." Buck pushed Marty toward a chair. "Now, Dale. You can't get protection without a police officer here to verify. You've got that. Spill. Who hired you?"

"I was hired by Dierks Carver."

"What?"

That wasn't the name Jeff was hoping for.

"He said he needed some help disrupting some things." Dale grimaced as he looked up at Buck. "We only did it because he said we didn't have to hurt anyone. I can't do that, hurt people like that."

"Who were you supposed to disrupt?"

Dale's gaze went back to Marty. "The TRT."

"Why?"

Dale's eyes darted between the men. "Look, I wasn't told everything. Dierks said when and where, who we needed to target. There was this girl we followed around a lot, and Dierks thought it was working great, making her nervous. Then we had to come here."

"To plant a phony bomb."

Dale nodded at Jeff. "See? I told you, we weren't in it to hurt anyone. But then, that girl got kidnapped and the police went crazy looking for us." Dale swallowed hard. "We were supposed to meet up one night, get paid. I'd met Dierks a few times, he seemed like a stand-up guy. Adil had worked for him a few times, odd jobs here and there. He always paid."

"Then he didn't?"

Sweat beaded Dale's upper lip as he slowly nodded to Marty. "When I got to the apartment, Adil and Thomas were already dead. It had to be Dierks, he was supposed to meet us there. So I took off."

"Did he say why you needed to disrupt us?" Buck questioned.

"He said, boss says we need to work harder to get the TRT out of the way. Make them look bad or take them out, your choice. So, we choose to make you look bad. Thomas has some experience in computers and started posting clusters of negative comments, disrupting public view."

"Computers, huh? What about hacking?" Buck gritted.

"I know he was doing a lot of stuff online, but he didn't say what. It was either for another job or maybe for this one? I'm not sure."

Jeff shook his head at the revelation. "Now we know where the leak came from."

"But it doesn't explain who paid them."

"Who was giving the orders?" Marty questioned.

"I don't know."

Marty's face went red. "I can arrest you and take you in right now."

"No! They'll kill me!"

"Who?" Buck leaned in. "Why do you keep saying that?"

Dale fidgeted with the water bottle in his hands. "Dierks mentioned we had inside help. There was no way we could get caught. That means cops were involved. No one ever showed up in time, we were out before it got bad every single time. But I don't know who, that's why I came here. I thought if I told you what I know, you'd be able to do enough digging and figure it out so they wouldn't kill me."

Jeff paced the room. "Do you have anything you can give us to prove what happened? Any emails, text messages, anything? Cause right now, blaming the police isn't enough to keep you safe."

Dale wiped his brow. "My old cell phone, I stashed it before I left." He pulled out a set of keys from his pocket. "It has everything Dierks ever texted me. Thomas said he had a way to find out who the boss was, who else Dierks was texting, but he would need Dierks's actual cell phone to do it. Maybe you can do that?"

Marty took the keys.

"Train station locker over on 12th."

———

AFTER PLACING Dale Fletcher in Evan's charge, Jeff, Buck, and Marty headed to the train station.

Sprinting inside, they turned down the wing with the lockers. Jeff surveyed the numbers and headed down the alley. "Here, number four-fourteen."

Marty unlocked the door and pulled out a bag with the cell phone inside. The old-school phone opened without a passcode, and they looked over the text messages.

Jeff nodded at the phone and Marty. "Call the number."

"But we know Dierks Carver is dead."

"Did they ever find his phone?" Buck asked.

"I don't recall, but it wasn't my case."

"Then we have a chance to either discover who might have his phone now or find where it is. Either way, it can lead to answers." Jeff glared at the detective.

Marty pushed in the name and waited. "Who's this?" His eyes widened as he stared between Jeff and Buck. "No, thanks. I just got the answers I needed." Hanging up, he looked to Jeff and Buck. "The phone we found on the dead guy from your doctor mishap, it rang to him. The officer in the evidence lockup answered."

"Ryan Cushing? So Ryan picked up where Dierks left off. That means someone is still paying to take us out. There's someone else."

"Ryan Cushing is dead, and the head of the cartel is under arrest. The FBI won't let us interrogate the cartel guy."

"You remember what Dani said?" Jeff turned to Buck. "The only one's benefitting from us going under are the bad guys. Maybe it's Ivanov."

"No, he can't get in with the locals here. It has to be a home-grown traitor."

Jeff frowned at Marty, but it did make sense. Ivanov was new to the area and yet well-known.

"The boss. The one calling the shots. And who would have the pull to disrupt police protection?" Buck glared up at Jeff. "Stonewall."

"Buck, don't even think it. You can't go after the commissioner with a hunch. You've got to have proof." Marty shook his head.

"It's not just him, there has to be someone else," Buck commented. "Frazier isn't the man I thought he was, but he'd never do this on his own. He's being led there. Let's get back."

Jeff mulled the information all the way back to the TRT to collect Dale Fletcher. If the commissioner was involved, there had to be someone else pushing his buttons.

But who else would have the money, the power?

42

"Can I have your attention?"

Two days since the rescue of Shelby and the arrest of the head of a major drug cartel, Jeff was still on edge and looking over his shoulder. Although Dale Fletcher was caught, they still had a missing player—or two. And without evidence against the commissioner, Marty wasn't about to commit political suicide going after the man without anything less than a bullet-proof case.

Jeff watched the press conference from the back of the room, his heart pounding and a churning in his gut. Mayor Bradley stood at the podium, cameras clicking away as Buck forced a smile and stood to the back of the mayor.

"I'd like to thank the Dallas SWAT team and the TRT for coming to the aid of the FBI in apprehending one of the deadliest drug cartels in the city."

An eruption in applause rang out as the mayor shook Buck's hand, then the SWAT team leader as well as the FBI agent.

"From what I've been told, more arrests will be made as the FBI's investigation into the rise of one of the deadliest cartels to invade our city is cleared up. We're going to rid our city of the drugs and criminals that reside here, and I'm proud to stand with all of these local agencies that work so well together."

As the clapping commenced, Buck made his way from the stage and to Jeff.

"You see Stonewall anywhere?"

Jeff straightened and glanced around the room. "No. He should be on that podium taking credit for the police and their involvement."

Buck shook his head. "Let's go."

With a frown, Jeff followed Buck out the door.

SHELBY STARED at the mirror in the bathroom, barely able to recognize her own face. The swelling had lessened thanks to the medication, but the bruising was extensive. Letting out a sigh, she finished packing her things and slowly made it back to her room.

After two days of sitting in bed, she'd had enough. A blow to the stomach, fatigue, and PTSD weren't reasons to stay in the hospital. Besides, all the help in the world wouldn't give her back any peace.

She'd almost gotten Jeff killed. It was one thing that she ended up back in trouble, but pulling Jeff in hurt her heart.

A knock made her jump.

"Come in," she stuttered, her voice still weak.

"Hey." Danica peeked around the corner. "Do you have a second?"

Shelby eased into the chair and took a deep breath. "Sure."

Danica placed a happy face mug filled with white and yellow daisies on the table in front of Shelby. "I didn't think you'd be leaving so soon."

"Well, I'll rest better at home, and that's what I need. There's not much they can do for me here." She smiled at the gift. "Thanks for the flowers."

"You're welcome." Danica sat down and crossed her legs, that inquisitive stare set on Shelby. "Do you remember when we talked and I told you that I trusted you to make the right decision?"

Shelby nodded.

"I think you're making the wrong one."

"Dani."

"Nope. Save your voice, I think you're going to need it later." Dani leaned in on her knees. "The thing is, I think you do know what the right decision is, but you're too afraid to make it. I'm not here to convince you to get back together with Jeff. I think that's what you want more than anything else in the world. I'm here to convince you to let go of whatever it is that's telling you it's all your fault."

"It is."

"It's Ryan's fault. It's that drug guy's fault. The guilt has nothing to do with you. You were the target, the victim, just like Jeff."

"If I had told Jeff about everything, then he would've known and—"

"And what? We both know that Jeff would've been in on this from the get-go. He never would've left you standing there without help. He loves you."

Shelby tried to swallow the lump in her throat as tears ran down her cheeks.

"Look, even if you'd told him the full extent of what had happened, you didn't know what was going to happen. This wasn't anything you were involved in voluntarily. We don't know how it would've played out. There was no proof it was your ex until he was there and it was too late."

As much as Shelby didn't want to sit there and say nothing, she couldn't get a word out.

"Just know that no one blames you. I sure don't, and you know Jeff doesn't. Buck's been worried to death too. None of us think you did the wrong thing." Danica twisted her fingers together, her diamond ring shining bright. "Trust is a funny thing. It seems so simple, yet we make it much more complicated than necessary.

"I didn't trust my team to think of me as who I am, not what I came from. I didn't trust Haiden with the truth for a really long time. Sometimes when you survive things that don't make sense, things you can't control, you feel as if there were something more you should've been able to do."

Danica headed for the door. "If you do want to talk or text, I'm free."

"Thanks," Shelby managed to whisper before Danica left the room.

43

"We can't just bust into the police commissioner's home. You get that, right?" Jeff muttered as Buck drove to the country club area of east Dallas.

"I do. But if he's not at that press conference, then he's probably being held up for a reason."

"How does it make any sense that the commissioner is involved? How does he fit? And what about Shelby?"

"She was just a pawn, a payoff. She said Ryan was trying to get in the good graces of the cartel. You mentioned he tried to get you to get on board too, right?"

Jeff hung on the car door as Buck took a hard right. "Yeah, he wanted me to give info on police activity, clear a path for them should we come knocking. Isn't that just part of the drug cartel and what they were hoping to create?"

"I think it's more." Buck shoved the SUV in park and slid from the vehicle.

Jeff sidled next to Buck as they edged around the back of the house. Yelling, screaming echoed from inside.

"Call it in. Let me see if I can stall them."

"Buck! Wait," Jeff hissed.

But it was too late. He was gone.

249

Jeff let his eyes adjust to the darkness in the garage. Gun ready, he eased his way from the door and through the breezeway. Already bypassing a man on the ground, he checked the downed man's pulse. Alive but unconscious.

Hearing muffled voices, he eased around the doorframe and into the hallway. Swinging his gun around, he blocked a blow, dropping his weapon in the process. Taking a hit to the face, he quickly recovered and swept the man's feet from under him, pinning him to the ground and knocking him out with a swift hit to the back of the head.

Wiping the blood trailing from his lip, Jeff stood and regained his weapon to continue his way through the hallway.

"I want what's mine!"

A familiar voice echoed through the massive home. Clearing the rooms as he went, Jeff hurried toward the lit room when another scream came through. He saw Buck leaned up against the wall, a finger to his lips.

"I did what I could! I had no idea before it was too late!" Frazier Stonewall's voice echoed, bargaining with his life. "I can still be an asset."

Jeff crept to the other side of the door as Buck counted down. At one, he shoved the door open and followed Buck into the room.

"Police! No one move!"

His jaw hit the ground to see Louis Roltz standing in front of the commissioner, a drink in his hand.

44

———

"Well, if it isn't the ranger cowboy," Louis mumbled as he turned. "And his sidekick friend. What's going on? You guys are the worst protection detail I've ever hired. Not just the one, but two guys through? Where's the rest of the team?"

"Want to fire them? I think they'd probably be willing to walk away right now." Buck's low voice rumbled through the silence.

Scoping the room, Jeff counted three men, two with guns aimed at him and Buck, one with his sleeves rolled up and blood splatter on his clothes.

"I knew you were part of this."

Louis chuckled and turned, perched on the edge of the desk. "Based on the look on your face when you walked in, I don't think you had any idea." He took a long drink from the glass in his hand. "By the way, you're outnumbered."

Buck swung his gun to Louis. "I know you don't care if I hit one of your guys, but you will care if I hit you. They shoot, you die."

"What about your friend? Don't you want to save his life?"

"I can handle myself," Jeff muttered.

"Not you. Him." Roltz motioned to the commissioner.

251

Buck eased around the room, as did Jeff, trying to gain a better angle and cover if needed.

"What friend?"

"The commish here. Aren't you two buddies?"

The man holding the commissioner hostage pulled out a knife, holding it to his throat.

Buck shrugged. "He's in on it. Helped to get Danica kidnapped. You could say we're no longer friendly."

"I didn't know, Buck. I didn't," the commissioner stuttered.

"Oh, come now, Frazier." Louis stood and paced the room. "Of course you did. This was the plan from the beginning. Disrupt the one team we couldn't control. The police were out of the way, but the TRT—they were becoming a problem. If I was going to ascend, then I needed them dismantled."

"It was all you," Jeff gritted out.

"Not really. I just helped where I could. I don't normally get my hands dirty, but when push comes to shove, I wasn't going to let anyone get in my way. But I did have some great help. Men that weren't concerned about getting their hands dirty."

"The run for the mayor. It was all about putting you in office."

"Mayor, then governor, then President. I'm working my way up." Louis winked at Jeff.

"Where did Dani fit in? The kidnapping?" Buck's face went red as Louis let out a grin.

"That was fate. I was already working an angle on her sister, hoping it would be enough to take her out. You and your friend there, you're not a team without her." Louis shrugged and poured another drink. "It was a shock to me when she went missing. But advantageous. If she had never come back, it would've cinched up my work."

"The cartel, they agreed to put you in power if you got rid of us." Buck's eyes narrowed. "The file. How did you get the file?"

"You'd have to talk to the dead man about that. All of them, actually. I have no idea where it came from or how they got it."

"Fletcher," Jeff mumbled. "He would know."

Louis's eyes narrowed as he set down his drink.

"He found us. Didn't think he could trust the cops. Now I know why." Buck took a few steps forward. "It's not just Frazier you have in your pocket, is it?"

Louis took out his own gun and aimed it Frazier, pulling the trigger.

"No!" Buck leaped forward, shoving the attacker with the knife into the line of fire.

Gunfire erupted and the familiar smell of tear gas filled the room. Coughing and wheezing, Jeff crawled to Buck, who was working on Frazier's bindings.

"Let's go," Jeff yanked at Buck's arm and helped drag Frazier from the room and out the side door.

Boots and tactical gear surrounded them as Jeff's gun was pulled from his hand and cuffs were tightened on his wrists.

"Why did you save me?" Frazier coughed and sputtered.

"You don't deserve this," Buck mumbled from the ground, also cuffed.

As the smoke began to clear, more sirens grew closer.

"Hey! Get those off." Special Agent Peters approached, motioning to Jeff and Buck. "You want to tell me how you got here first?"

Buck coughed and took a few deep breaths, rubbing his wrists. "Give me my gun back and we'll talk."

Jeff rolled to his back a moment, taking a few deep breaths as Buck appeared overhead.

"You shot?" He pulled at Jeff's left arm.

Jeff looked down, tugging at the sleeve. "Just a scratch. Probably a ricochet from one of the shots."

"You shouldn't have followed me in. I was already outnumbered. You should've waited for the FBI." He extended a hand and Jeff took it.

Jeff shook his head as he stood, trying to clear it from the fumes.

"What made you go in?" Peters asked.

"I've known Frazier for a long time. He's always in the mood for recognition. If he wasn't at the conference, then he had to be up to something else."

"But that doesn't explain why you went in." Jeff crossed his arms. "Like you said, you were outnumbered."

"He was a friend. He didn't deserve to be tortured like that. I wasn't going to let them kill him when I could stop it." Buck watched them walk Louis Roltz out in handcuffs. "Did you know about Roltz?"

"We had our suspicions. We've put guys on him, tried getting info from his people, but no one ever talked. We finally linked him to Ivanov, so we were headed this way."

"Ivanov? How?" Jeff questioned.

"Phone records and some texts. We went through the heist at the clinic and a Detective DeSalis mentioned a phone on one of the deceased. It had a trove of information from a blocked number. My guys were able to get a trace on it and it led to Roltz's office, so we got a warrant. There was a burner cell in his desk with all the info. We traced his other phone and came here."

"Good thing you did. You've got great timing." Jeff chuckled.

"I'm going to check on Frazier."

Jeff watched Buck attempt to console his old friend.

"About that story."

He turned to Peters.

"We've already spoken to the reporter. It's been listed as a national security incident and if anything is leaked about what happened, she'll face a maximum security imprisonment."

"But it's true, right?"

"He's never told you?"

"Buck doesn't talk shop. I've only heard bits and pieces about his buddies, friends he knows. But nothing else."

Peters' jaw clenched. "My uncle was part of that unit."

Jeff drew in a breath.

"It wasn't Buck's fault. It was a raid, bad intel—you name it, it happened. The only way Buck survived was instinct and the hand of God. I've done a lot of digging on that mission, trying to figure it out. But all I know is that Buck Thompson went back and carried every single man out of that trench once he finished his duty."

Jeff swallowed hard, glancing up at his mentor. "He's never left anyone behind. When his brother died, he could've walked away from Dani and her sister and mother. But he took care of them." He shook his head. "He could've walked away from me."

Peters slapped his arm as he walked by. "People survive for a reason. I guess you've figured out why he did."

Buck returned, his jaw set.

"Did he say why?"

"He said he didn't have a choice. Roltz had him on the line for some embezzlement."

"What you found on his hard drive?"

Buck nodded. "If it came to light, he'd be in prison, and his life would be over."

"It's over now."

"Sometimes men grasp at whatever will keep them afloat, not realizing it will drag them down later on." Buck let out a breath. "Let's get your arm cleaned up and go check on the team."

"My arm's fine."

Buck gave him a steely glare. "Don't argue, Jeff."

"Yes, sir."

45

Shelby paced her bedroom, shivering and gripping her phone to her chest.

For two days, she'd been struggling to sleep, waking with dreams and wanting so badly to call Jeff.

He'd texted a few times to check on her, asked if she wanted or needed anything. But she couldn't make herself text back.

The fact was, she wanted him, needed him to come find her, scoop her up and take it all away. The fear, the pain, the hurt, and the disappointment. It overwhelmed her every day and night. It took all her energy to get up out of bed anymore.

She jumped as her phone rang. Jeff's name flashed across the screen.

"Hello?"

"Hey. Didn't know if you'd pick up."

She opened her mouth to speak, but she couldn't make her voice work.

"Shelby? I called because I've been worried sick and I want to make sure you're okay. If you can't handle any of the other stuff, I don't care right now. I just ... I need to know you're okay."

Closing her eyes, she slid to the ground. "I'm not," she whispered.

"What can I do?"

"I don't know," she mumbled between tears, wiping her face and trying to keep from completely breaking down.

"Would you be upset if I came by?"

She stood and pulled back part of the blinds from the bedroom window. Jeff's truck was parked outside her house.

"You mad?"

Her chuckle slipped out. The truck door immediately opened and Jeff slid down.

"I'm hoping that means you'll open the door."

She dropped her phone on the bed and rushed to the front. As she unlocked and opened it, Jeff swept her up in a hug. Somehow the door shut, but between her tears and the exhaustion, she couldn't even stand.

Gripping his neck, she found herself sitting on his lap in the living room, curled against his chest. His hands rubbed her back, and she relaxed for the first time in a week.

"You're not sleeping, are you?"

She shook her head.

"You could've called. Any time, you know that," he whispered.

Sitting back, she wiped her face as Jeff pushed her hair behind her ear. "Jeff, I ..."

He kissed her cheek. "I love you, Shelby. I'm not going anywhere, no matter how long it takes for you to find a way to forgive yourself."

Her eyes closed as his breath hit her neck. She shivered.

"Cold?"

She pushed into the crook of his neck. His arms wrapped her up. It took only a few minutes before her body eased and she fell asleep.

JEFF RELAXED INTO THE CUSHIONS, holding onto Shelby. *Thanks, Lord.*

She'd been out for almost an hour, and he was happy to sit and hold her all night if it would help her sleep. He knew she was done the moment she fell into his arms. Between the trauma she'd been through and the physical harm, it was no wonder she'd fallen asleep so quickly.

Had she even heard his words?

Not being able to hold on to her and help her through this, he'd make sure to repeat it over and over again until she understood. He loved her more than he could put into words.

Her body tensed.

"Shelby?"

She pushed up with wide eyes.

"It's okay. You're okay."

"What? I'm sorry. I fell asleep."

"I know. I was hoping you would." He pushed her hair from her shoulder. Frowning at the bruise next to her eye, he sighed. "How's your head?"

She fingered the sore spot. "It's okay." Her eyes searched his. "How are you?"

"I'm much better now." He kissed her forehead.

"I'm so sorry, Jeff," she whispered.

"I know, but you don't have to be. None of this is on you. Please stop asking for forgiveness that isn't needed."

"But I hid all of it. I was too ashamed and embarrassed to tell you. I was going to, after you told me everything, but I just couldn't make myself."

He held a finger to her lips. "Shelby. I forgive you for not telling me about it. But not telling me didn't lead to what happened to us. It would've happened either way."

Her brows furrowed a moment.

"Now, are you hungry? You want me to order some food?"

"What?"

"You need to get your strength up. I need a date to a wedding."

Shelby's jaw dropped.

"It's in two weeks. I'm pretty sure all that bruising will be gone and I'm not about to take another no for an answer. I'm not leaving again. And I'm sure not going to the wedding without you."

"But your friends, and what happened—"

"I heard Danica paid you a visit?"

She nodded.

"Then you know none of them blame you for any of it. Like I said, it happened because it happened. We did all we could to protect you, keep you safe, and I'm sorry we failed."

"You didn't fail."

He sighed, wrapping both his arms around her waist. "We did. It was our job, my job, to keep you safe. I failed you."

"Jeff, please. It's not your fault, I took off and ran outside without you." Tears streamed down her red cheeks.

Wiping them away, he smirked. "If you really forgive me, you'll come to the wedding with me."

Her eyes went wide. "You're going to negotiate a date with me?"

He shrugged. "Doesn't seem to be working any other way." Pulling her in for a hug, he gently kissed her cheek. "I love you, Shelby. I'm not going anywhere, and I'm just going to wait around for you to say yes. Might as well say it now."

"Yes to what?" she whispered.

A shudder ran down his spine. "Let's start with the date to the wedding, and we can go from there."

She snuggled once more into his arms, his heart pounding.

46

Jeff held on to Shelby's hand, refusing to let her go. The wedding was finally over and he'd barely been able to take in a breath at the sight of Shelby Durning all dressed up and walking his way. There was no way anyone in the building would think she was there alone.

"You okay? You're staring again." Shelby narrowed her eyes.

Leaning in, he gave her a gentle kiss. "I'm great. How are you?"

Her amber eyes danced back and forth, a smile growing on her face. "I'm glad you asked me to come."

"I'm glad you finally relented."

With a chuckle, she wrapped an arm around his waist. Shelby hanging onto him was about the best feeling in the world. Especially when she was smiling and happy.

"You want to dance?"

She looked up with wide yes. "You dance?"

He scoffed and set down his punch. "Of course. I'm an amazing dancer." Taking her cup, he sat it down and pulled her to the dance floor.

Grinning at the laughter from spinning her around, he pulled her in close.

"Have I ever told you how amazing you are?"

She sighed. "Jeff."

"You are an amazing woman." Giving her a kiss on the cheek, he smiled at how her shoulder shrugged and goosebumps spread across her bare arms. "Cold?"

"No, not at all." Her arms went around his neck as she leaned into his body.

"I love you, Shelby."

She tensed for a moment.

It was taking all he had not to convince her she felt the same way. It was more than obvious the way she looked up at him, kissed him, held his hand so firmly in hers. But he wouldn't push, not this time. For the first time in forever, he was more than willing to wait her out, let her figure it out on her own.

"This is a wonderful day," she whispered.

He nodded.

"Are you all right?"

With a chuckle, he pulled her back, holding her face in his hand. "I've got the most beautiful woman dancing with me, and I think I might be able to snag a kiss later this evening from her. I'm perfect."

She chuckled and pushed up, planting a gentle kiss on his lips. "You didn't have to wait."

"Good to know." With a grin, he led her from the dance floor and to the far side of the room, eager for some time alone and, hopefully, another kiss.

BUCK STOOD at the back of the wedding reception.

Watching his team, he smiled at the different journeys they'd taken to make it here. They'd all survived so much, sacrificed so much, to find a place where they belonged.

That's what made the TRT so important. It wasn't just his

new family. It was a home for those that needed it. Family and support when surviving wasn't enough.

As Bexley and Evan enjoyed their dance, Sergio and his wife Tamara watched with smiles on their faces. Haiden and Danica stood to the side, completely focused on each other and ignoring the chaos around them, knowing their day was fast approaching.

And then there was Jeff. Holding onto a smiling Dr. Shelby Durning, it was more than obvious where they were finally headed.

"I came to give life and give it abundantly," Buck murmured.

His savior's words filled his heart. It wasn't enough to just live this life, go through the motions without pause for why they were here. They were all given a choice, a choice to accept grace and mercy and use it to make this world better, make their own lives better.

For the first time in years, it was if Jesus was finally showing him why he survived that terrible day, why his life was spared. And for the first time since that night, Buck felt peace surrounding him.

EPILOGUE

Sitting in the gazebo, Shelby smiled as Haiden and Danica opened their gifts.

Bexley had decided that, despite their elopement, the two deserved a wedding shower. Haiden's parents had come, as well as the entire TRT. The gazebo was covered in lights, balloons, and a large *Congratulations Mr. & Mrs. Blake* banner.

"How are you?"

She grinned as Jeff came from behind and sat down, giving her a quick kiss on the cheek.

"I'm good. This was a wonderful idea."

"Bexley was adamant, even though I have a feeling Dani will be ready to leave just as soon as the cake is served."

She chuckled, sipping her punch.

Jeff took hold of her hand, giving it a squeeze.

After six weeks of therapy and finally getting back to work, the fear and failure that plagued her constantly were easing. Her entire world had crumbled once more, and if she hadn't had friends and therapy to keep her steady, she would've folded like last time. Then there was Jeff.

She smiled at his handsome profile, his hand gripping hers. He never backed down, even on those days she really wanted him to leave. When she'd have a bad night that morphed into a worse day, he'd swoop in and pull her from the house for a game night and pizza at his office with the rest of the group. Instead of the nightmare she'd imagined once her secret was out, he'd become a bulwark holding her up and keeping her safe.

Music drifted from the speakers, and Haiden led Danica to the middle of the gazebo for a dance. Bexley and Evan soon joined and Jeff stood.

"Come on."

Heat rising on her face, she allowed Jeff to pull her to the floor, wrapping his arm around her waist.

"You okay?

"Yes. Why?"

"You get jumpy when the subject of marriage comes up."

"I do not." She scowled as he let out a chuckle. "Besides, no one is talking marriage. They're already married."

"What if I wanted to talk about it?"

Swallowing the lump forming in her throat, she let out a sigh. "I'm not sure this is the best time."

"I always have good timing. You know that better than anyone."

"Jeff, things are finally starting to ease up. Maybe that's enough for now."

He pulled her in tight, her cheek barely brushing his even with her heels on. As they swayed back and forth, the tightness in her chest diminished with each breath.

"I love you, Shelby."

"I love you too."

"You think now's the time to finally say that?" Pulling her back, his ice-blue eyes stared into hers. "It's been a long time coming."

"Yes, it has. I want you to know that I do love you, Jeff. Not because you saved my life, not because you've lifted me up from my worst and stuck with me through all the chaos. I love you because you're you."

His eyes cut back and forth as he watched her.

"You know I can make that decision myself, right?"

He nodded, tucking some stray hair behind her ear. "You're pretty amazing, Shel."

She huffed. "I'm not so sure about that."

Leaning in, he gave her a gentle kiss.

"Hey, we're cutting the cake, in case you didn't notice."

Shelby's eyes went wide as Evan's voice cut through the music. Pulling Jeff around, they stood to the side as Haiden and Danica shared a piece of cake.

Jeff's arm worked its way around Shelby's waist.

"Thanks, everyone. We appreciate all this." Danica's cheeks burned red as Haiden kept hold.

"We're so happy for you." Bexley gave Danica a hug as Buck shook Haiden's hand.

The couple made their way around the group, pausing at Shelby.

"Congratulations," Shelby grinned.

Danica pulled her in for a hug. "I'm so glad you're back."

Shelby chuckled. "I'm not sure about back. But I'm better."

"Not what I meant." Danica winked and handed her a small bouquet.

"What's this?"

"Since my sister got sick and couldn't make it, you're the only single woman here. Instead of throwing it, I decided I'd just hand it off."

Jeff came up behind her with a laugh. "What's that?"

"Just a little gift." Danica grabbed Jeff in a hug.

"I'm sure she appreciates it." He winced as Danica punched his arm. "Easy."

"Be nice," Danica muttered.

"Thanks."

As the new couple left, Jeff wrapped Shelby up.

"That's a wonderful bouquet. Doesn't that mean you're the next one to get married?"

"Well, since I'm the only single woman here, that would make sense."

"Come on." He took her hand and led her away from the gazebo as everyone else began to clean up.

"We should stay and help."

"We'll go back in a minute."

"Jeff, don't you dare ..."

He chuckled and pulled her around in front of him. Leaning in, he gave her a deep kiss, pushing the bounds of intimacy. Pulling back, she stared up, her breath heavy.

"What are you doing?"

With a shrug, he fingered her jaw. "Shelby, I do want to marry you one day. I just want to know if that's what you want too."

Attempting to take in a breath, easing the pounding of her heart in her ears, she forced her mind to stop swimming. "One day, I do want to marry you. But right now, I just want to survive," she whispered.

Wiping tears that suddenly appeared on her cheeks, Jeff frowned. "You're not surviving, Shelby. Can't you see that? You're thriving. You smile more now."

She couldn't hold back as he grinned. "I have a lot more to smile about than I used to." She wrapped him in a hug, her arms around his neck as he swayed back and forth.

Urgency gripped her heart. The mistakes in her life, the times she came so close to death, all added up so quickly in her mind. She'd prayed often for God to open the right doors, to lead her down the right paths. In the past few months, those paths always led to Jeff.

He stuck around through all of it, gave her strength, and led her closer to God. They went to church every week if they were both free from work, studying together and going to Bible studies. He'd brought a sense of peace into her life that had been missing for so long.

Easing back, she studied his amazing blue eyes. Pulling him

in, she offered another kiss. Earth shaking moments later, his echoing breath sounded in her ear.

"And what was that for?" he whispered.

"An answer."

He stepped back. "An answer?"

Holding the bouquet in front of her, she smiled as Jeff's face lit up. "I'm thinking a June wedding, next year."

He pulled her in for another kiss. "You just tell me where and when. I'll be there."

"You know you do have to actually propose at some point, right?"

With a chuckle, he leaned to her ear. "I've had a ring picked out for months, just waiting on you."

Heart pounding, she wrapped her arms around his neck and held on. "I love you, Jeff Powers."

"I love you, Shelby."

ACKNOWLEDGMENTS

I want to thank my publishing company for helping me through this series. You've all been so great to direct my ramblings into a storyline that can be followed and understood! I appreciate your work and willingness to allow me time to get through the final edits and get this novel completed.

OTHER BOOKS IN THE TACTICAL RESPONSE TEAM SERIES

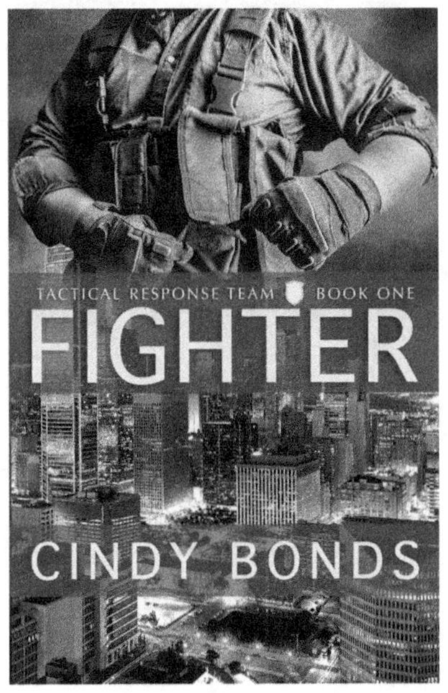

Fighter

Book One of the Tactical Response Team (TRT)

https://scrivenings.link/fighter

Book Two of the Tactical Response Team (TRT)

https://scrivenings.link/protector

OTHER BOOKS BY CINDY BONDS

Rainstorm

by Cindy Bonds

Laurel Ashburn has a scarred past, filled with corruption and pain. After an injury overseas sends her home, she moves back in with her foster mother and to a town that hates her. Being home puts her on a path to find a missing friend. But when she's attacked over and over, who will be willing to help?

Detective Dev Hollister traded in the big city for a slower pace and less crime in rural Arkansas. After rescuing Laurel from an attempted kidnapping, he finds himself intrigued with this headstrong and stubborn woman.

While Dev's job is to protect Laurel, he wants much more than to solve the case. He wants to give her a new life and reason to stay.

Laurel will have to push beyond her dark past to trust Dev with her life. But after losing so much, can Laurel survive one more storm?

Hostage

by Cindy Bonds

Her confidence shot, Agent Macy Packer desperately wants to go back to her regular life, before she was taken hostage. To forget the pain, the fear and forget the man that helped her through all of it, then disappeared.

Kane Bledsoe is finally healed, his scars serving as a reminder of his time in captivity. But all he can think about is the blue-eyed woman that saved him. She had saved them all and left him with a burning hope.

A chance meeting and an attack prove Macy is still in danger. Kane pushes himself into the investigation, doing what he can to provide protection.

The enemy is clear, he wants Macy.

Kane will have to decide just how far he's willing to go to protect her. Can he sacrifice himself when the time comes?

Not a Good Day for Namaste

by Keri Lynn

A Texas-Sized Mystery - Book Two

Witnessing the hit and run of fellow Flamingo Springs resident Ryan wasn't how yoga instructor Misty Van Oepen planned on starting the Thanksgiving holidays.

When Ryan's mysterious brother shows up along with a spree of crime, she decides it's up to her and fellow business owners Lacey and Jeni, to find out what's going on. After an attempt on Misty's life lands her in protective custody at deputy Stetson Owens' ranch, she finds herself in danger of losing her heart to the former bull rider.

With time running out, will Misty succeed in discovering who's behind the attacks? Or will she fail and become the next victim?

The Plot Thickens

by Susan Page Davis

Skirmish Cove Mysteries - Book Two

Jillian only wants to redecorate one room at the Novel Inn—

but first she has to deal with murder.

Murder strikes Skirmish Cove during the coastal town's winter carnival. Jillian Tunney, part owner of the nearby Novel Inn, discovers the body of a clerk at her favorite bookstore. With her sister Kate and brother, Officer Rick Gage, she tries to find out who killed him.

Meanwhile, Jillian is immersed in redecorating one of the themed rooms, but Kate is annoyed when a mysterious guest at the inn doesn't want to leave his room. The innkeepers find they have way too many secrets to solve.

The Case of the Innocent Husband

by Deborah Sprinkle

A Mac & Sam Mystery - Book One

Private Investigator Mackenzie Love needs to do one thing. Find out who shot Eleanor Davis. Or else.

When Eleanor Davis is found shot in her garage, the only suspect, her estranged husband, is found not guilty in a court of law. However, most of the good citizens of Washington, Missouri, remain unconvinced. It doesn't matter that twelve men and women of the jury found him not guilty. What do they know?

And since Private Investigator Mackenzie Love accepted the job for the defense and helped acquit Connor Davis, her friends and neighbors have placed her squarely in the enemy camp. Therefore, her overwhelming goal becomes to find out who killed Eleanor Davis.

Or leave the town she grew up in.

As the investigation progresses, the threats escalate. Someone wants to stop Mackenzie and her partner, Samantha Majors, and is willing to do whatever it takes—including murder.

Can Mac and Sam find the killer before they each end up on the wrong side of a bullet?

www.ingramcontent.com/pod-product-compliance
Lightning Source LLC
Chambersburg PA
CBHW070627100726
47907CB00007B/1892